FIRENZE

Cover design and typesetting by Geoffrey Bunting
Cover image by Brent Granby

ISBN 978-1-967756-04-9

First Edition

Published by Otis West
OtisWestBooks.com

Author's Note

I wrote this novel during lunch breaks while working at a corporate job in Seattle in the early 2000s. Intended as a whimsical take on my own semester abroad in the late 80s, it is presented here in its original form—a time capsule from a bygone era.

FIRENZE

A NOVEL

OTIS WEST

One

We'd left the famous part of Florence with the Duomo and whatnot. Then we went through the more normal part—without all the famous stuff, but still kind of nice and Italian looking. Now we seemed to be in the shit part. This definitely wasn't the Italy you see in guidebooks. We were passing one ugly concrete building after another. It might as well have been Baltimore for all I knew.

I wasn't too sure about this cab driver. Did he even know where he was going? Maybe he'd misread the address I'd given him. Maybe he was crazy. Maybe I should have studied Italian a bit harder so I could ask him where the hell we were going.

The guy who'd driven me in from the airport the night before had at least known some English. He'd gotten really excited when he found out I was from California and kept asking if I'd met various movie stars—Arnold Schwarzenegger, Tom Cruise, Julia Roberts. But this dude I'd found today didn't know any English. He did have some serious bedhead, though—he had this shelf of hair coming out the side of his head that was all greasy and flecked with dandruff. It was kind of impressive.

I'd spent the night in a cheap pensione behind the Duomo. I was jet lagged and I ended up being kept awake half the night by a bunch of kids screaming and revving up their crappy mopeds in the street below. I finally fell asleep just as the sun started coming up, and then I overslept massively. When I woke up it was well past noon. I'd missed checkout, and when I rushed to the overseas study building, I learned I'd also missed the first big lunch. The administrator lady told me my roommate had gone ahead to our new host family without me. She gave me my host family's address and told me to be back the next day for the formal orientation. I took the address and went back outside and found this cab with bedhead guy.

The meter was already up to 7,450. I was still trying to figure out the money I'd changed at the airport. The 1000 lire notes were really small. The 50,000 notes were big and colorful. I knew what the conversion was but I was having a hard time doing the math in my head.

My finger was throbbing. I'd broken the index finger on my left hand three days before while skateboarding. It was taped into this aluminum cast thing with a bunch of blue foam that was starting to stink. My mom had tried to get me to not bring my skateboard to Italy, but I'd brought it anyway. I'd strapped it to the back of my backpack with a couple of bungees. I'd packed an extra set of wheels and bearings, too. Skating looked like it would be pretty shitty here, though. Too many cobblestones. But I'd probably find some places to skate. It was actually looking more encouraging the farther we got from "Centro."

After another few miles (kilometers?) of Baltimore we came to a stop in front of yet another large gray apartment building. The driver started fiddling with his meter.

"Esta qui?" I said.

The guy turned around and stared at me.

Shit! I'd lapsed into my high school Spanish again. I kept doing that for some reason. I guess "Senior Miller" had taught me something after all...

"Siamo qui?" I said.

"Si."

I looked at the apartment building again. It couldn't be right. I was supposed to be in a villa or something. I showed him the address again: 820 Via De Langhe.

He nodded. "Si, si." Then he told me the amount. I had no idea what he said but luckily I could read it for myself. The number on the meter had jumped up to 12,430. I handed the driver a crisp 50,000 and he gave me back a bunch of small, crumpled bills. Then I opened the door, stepped out and pulled my backpack out after me. I shut the door and the cab drove away.

I found Sr. Gasperi on the list of names next to the door buzzer. So this was the right place after all.

I hit the buzzer and waited. Nothing. I hit the buzzer again. Then again. I pushed it and held it. I held it until I started feeling stupid and then I let go. Still nothing. Crap, now what?

I stepped back to look up but couldn't see anyone except some lady shaking out a rug on a balcony a few floors up. Suddenly, the door buzzed. I lunged forward and caught it just in time. My backpack slid off my shoulder and smashed my knee.

The entranceway was dark and smelled like boiled cabbage. There was a small marble table and a few random pieces of mail scattered around on the floor.

I lugged my backpack up four flights of stairs, watching the numbers as I went. Then I came to a landing with the door partially open. Some dude was hanging back behind the door, smoking.

"Ciao?" I said.

The smoking guy came forward and said, "Americani?"

"Si," I said.

He nodded, then turned and walked back into the apartment. He was wearing jeans and a t-shirt and black socks with holes on the heels. I followed him down a long dark hallway, toward the sound of television.

Mid-way down the hall he stopped, pushed a door open and then reached into the room and switched on the light. He took another drag on his cigarette, then said a bunch of stuff I didn't understand. We stared at each other for a minute. He had a chicken pox scar in the middle of his forehead. I thought he looked a bit like Malcolm Young on the cover of Highway to Hell. I was tempted to tell him this, but instead I said, "Grazie."

He shrugged, then turned and walked down the hallway and disappeared into the room with the television. The door closed behind him.

I walked into the room. My roommate had staked out the bed near the balcony. I hadn't met him yet but apparently his name was Gary and he was from Colorado College. He'd left his suitcase open on the bed, stuck an alarm clock on the bedside table, and arranged his various shoes neatly on the floor: Nike running shoes, penny loafers, flip flops. All I had was one beat up pair of Vans. I probably should have bought a new pair before leaving for Italy, but oh well.

So I was stuck with the bed over in the corner, wedged between the door and this huge, medieval-looking cabinet. I dropped my backpack on the bed and walked out onto the balcony.

The apartment building across the way was identical, other than the fact that several floors had collapsed and there was a bunch of rebar and stuff hanging out. It looked like a bomb had hit the place.

There was a wooden bench on the balcony, along with several dead potted plants and a few red plastic crates filled with empty San Pellegrino bottles. Carbonated water seemed to be what everyone drank here. The stuff gave me a sore throat and these insane uncontrollable burps that came out my nose and hurt. I'd only been in the country like twelve hours and it was getting to be a major issue. I wanted something real to drink. Like some regular water or a Coke or something.

I walked back into the room and sat on my bed. So I was really here. I was really in Italy.

It was funny. It had been a somewhat random decision. I'd wanted to get out of Davis for a while. I'd already taken a quarter of Italian to satisfy the language requirement for the English major, and Florence was the easiest study abroad program to get into. So I signed up. Now I was here.

The one weird thing was that the daughter of my dad's new girlfriend was in the program, too. Some brainiac chick who went to Reed. I'd met her once at Christmas. She seemed ok, I guess. I didn't really care.

It had been a strange summer, too. I'd had a really awkward breakup with my long-time girlfriend, Kate. We'd dated on and off since senior year of high school. It seemed like it was finally off. I was glad. Sort of. Anyway, I was ready for something new. I just wasn't sure that this was it.

Two

I hadn't had a shower since I left the United States so I thought that would be a good thing to do next. The host family lady had left out some pink towels for us on our beds. They were worn and stiff and had a sour bleach smell.

I opened my backpack to get out some fresh clothes. My toothpaste had exploded in the middle of the backpack on the plane. I couldn't believe that one tube of toothpaste could cause that much havoc.

I dug around and found my soap dish, then pulled out some clothes that didn't seem to have any Aqua-Fresh on them. Then I took my stiff, stinky towel and walked out into the hall. The TV was still blasting down the hall.

The bathroom was directly across from our room. The toilet was kind of funky—the tank was up near the ceiling and there was a long chain hanging down. There was almost no water in the toilet bowl, which seemed to be the way they did it in Italy. After you take a crap you're supposed to scrub it with this brush they leave next to the toilet. I guess it saves water but it's pretty nasty.

There was no shower—there was just a tub. I don't think I'd taken a bath in a tub since I was like four years old with my plastic dinosaurs.

The tub looked pretty disgusting. There were rings around the edges and what looked like a big rust stain near the faucet. There was an attachment on the end of the faucet with a long hose with a shower nozzle thingy on the end of it. It looked like I was going to have to squat in the tub and give myself a shower.

I turned on the water and tried rinsing the tub a bit. It didn't do much good. Also, the water didn't seem to be getting warm. There appeared to be a mini water heater over in the corner. There was a little red light on it but who knows what that meant.

Screw it. I undressed and got into the tub. Then I squatted and shot freezing cold water on myself. I was shivering and trying to hold the nozzle and soap myself at the same time. My legs started to cramp up from squatting, but I didn't want to sit down cause the tub looked skuzzy as hell. I kept accidentally shooting water onto the wall and the floor.

And then someone started knocking on the door.

"Yeah?" I said.

A bunch of Italian.

"Hold on a second."

I got out shivering and still somewhat soapy and wrapped myself in the towel. The towel was too small so I had to hold it with one hand to keep it from falling off. I opened the door.

It was that Malcolm Young-looking guy again. He started saying a bunch of stuff I couldn't understand.

"Non capisco," I said.

He frowned.

I noticed that he had changed into a t-shirt that said "Fantastic!" I pointed to his shirt and said, "Fantastic!"

He looked vaguely annoyed. Then he said a bunch more stuff I didn't understand. I still didn't get it. He just shook his head and walked away.

I went back to my room and got dressed. I didn't feel clean at all. If anything I felt worse than before, since I was soapy and cold and now my skin smelled like a sour towel.

I was starting to get really hungry. We had been told that raiding the fridge was against the rules. The host family was supposed to provide us with breakfast and dinner and that was it. We were on our own for everything else.

I decided to go out and try to find some food. I also needed to call my mom and let her know I'd survived the trip.

I wondered what my roommate Gary was doing. I looked in his suitcase. It was packed with a bunch of preppy looking clothes, plus a Frisbee. Which was lamer, a Frisbee or a skateboard?

Three

I didn't know if I was supposed to have a key or how the whole in/out thing was supposed to work. But I decided that I should probably tell that Malcolm guy I was leaving. I walked down the hall and knocked on the door of the room where the TV sound was coming from. No answer.

"Hello?" I said. I knocked again. Still nothing. I decided to just open the door.

The Malcolm dude was sitting on this small leather couch watching some kind of talk show. He had about four pairs of shoes laid out on the floor in front of him and seemed to be in the middle of polishing them. He looked pretty surprised to see me.

I said, "Sono andiamo a centro." (I'd looked this up in my pocket dictionary beforehand.)

He just stared at me.

"Um, autobus?" I said. "Downtown?"

"Autobus?"

"Si, autobus?"

He said a bunch of stuff I didn't catch.

"Okay," I said. "Grazie."

He just stared at me some more.

I said, "Ciao," then walked out and closed the door behind me.

I crossed the street to the bus stop. I had looked at a bus map and was pretty sure this would get me in the right direction. I stood in front of a small clothing store that appeared to be closed. Maybe they were out of business. There was another store next door that sold weird metal implements. It looked like surgical equipment or something. It also was either closed or out of business.

Amazingly, a bus came. It was orange. I got on and said, "Centro?"

"Si," the driver said.

Hey, maybe I was doing okay with this Italian stuff after all.

The orientation packet had explained the whole bus thing. You bought bus tickets at cafes, and then you punched them when you got on the bus. You were supposed to keep your ticket in case an inspector came on the bus and asked to see it. The administrator lady at the center had given me some tickets for free. I took one of my tickets out and went and punched it in the little machine in back of the bus. Then I sat down near a bunch of middle-aged women with weird-looking stockings and ugly shoes. A few other people got on the bus at the next stop but no one punched their ticket. Maybe they had monthly passes or something.

After a while we left Baltimore and it started looking like we were in Italy again. And then we were back in the main part of Florence with a bunch of Americans walking around looking confused. I got off the bus near the train station.

I was starving. I couldn't figure what else to do so I went and got some gelato at one of these touristy places across from the Duomo. They have some seriously good ice-cream in Italy. Especially the weird nut flavors. So I ate a second one and then I felt sick.

I had a little map showing where the American Express office was, where the post office was, and where you went to make long distance phone calls. So I went to the phone place and got in a long line. I ended up behind two American college girls who were talking about all the leather crap they were going to buy. After a while the one with scary-looking nails noticed me and asked me what program I was with.

I said, "Non parlo Inglese."

The other one who was wearing these huge Jackie-O sunglasses laughed and said, "You're not Italian."

I just shrugged.

They both laughed and then whispered something to each other and nodded. I pretended to look around.

Finally it was my turn. When the chicks weren't looking I had been secretly studying my phrase book so I would know what to say, but the guy didn't give me a chance—he just pointed me down the hallway. I walked down the hall until I came to this row of booths. I went into one of them and closed the door. Then I dialed home.

My brother answered. He's sixteen and his hormones were raging so he always acted like a total retard.

"Dude, what's up? How's Italy?"

"Alright."

"Are the chicks hot?"

"I guess. Where's mom?"

"You guess? What do you mean you guess?"

"Just let me talk to mom."

"She went out to buy a new toaster."

"What? Why?"

"The old one caught on fire."

"What?"

"Yeah, a bagel got stuck in there and I guess it didn't shut off like it was supposed to and it totally started burning. It made a huge black mark on the ceiling and everything."

"Oh," I said.

My brother said, "What time is it there?"

"Around five," I said.

"At night?"

"Yeah."

"Oh."

There was a long silence. I could hear fish swimming around in the Atlantic Ocean.

"Well, tell mom I called," I said.

"Alright," he said.

"Later," I said, and hung up.

Outside this huge crowd of Hare Krishnas was walking down the street—with the orange robes and funny haircuts. They looked just like the ones I'd seen in the Chicago airport when making my transfer. Maybe they were the same ones. Maybe they were on vacation. But then I heard them speaking Italian. Italian Hare Krishnas. That seemed kind of cool.

I walked around for a while. Most of the stores that didn't sell tourist crap were closed. I wondered when Italians actually bought anything.

I kept having to step off the sidewalk to get around packs of tourists, but then every time I stepped into the street I'd almost be run over by some kid on a moped. I was really getting sick of these kids on their mopeds. They were everywhere. They were either trying to run you down or they were hanging out in these little packs—just sitting on their mopeds with the kickstands on. Seemed like all the kids here dressed the same—with blue jeans and blue shoes and neon-colored backpacks. They looked dorky as hell.

I decided to go back to the program center, just to see if anyone was around or if I was missing anything.

The center was on the other side of the Ponte Vecchio—that covered bridge that you see in every tourist photo of Florence. Walking across it is a pain in the ass cause it's so packed with tourists buying tourist crap.

The center building itself was in some huge palace that was like five hundred years old. It was weird to think that when it was built Columbus hadn't even infected a bunch of Indians with smallpox or whatever. Or maybe he had. But George Washington definitely hadn't chopped down the cherry tree yet. This building was probably already on its third remodel by then.

I walked up the huge steps and through the big doors.

The first person I saw was this chick Trish from Davis. We knew each other vaguely from freshman year. I don't think she liked me much, but here we acted like long lost friends.

"Trish," I said. "What's up?"

"Hey Kevin!"

Hugs.

She wasn't looking too good. A bit too skinny and a bit too tan. Did she get a nose job?

"They lost my luggage," she said.

"That sucks."

"They're supposed to deliver it to me tomorrow."

"Oh, that's cool."

"Have you met your host family yet?"

"Yeah," I said. "Kind of."

"How are they?"

"I don't know. Okay I guess. What about you?"

"Oh, they are so nice. And the house is incredible. It's only like two blocks from here."

"You're lucky. I have to ride the bus for like half an hour."

"Oh, right, I heard you're with Gary."

"I guess. I haven't met him yet."

"He's really nice."

"Huh."

She seemed to be considering something. "Some of us are going to meet up later."

"Yeah?"

"Yeah, we're going to meet in front of the Duomo at nine. Maybe go out for drinks. You should come."

"I'll try to make it. I'm still figuring out the bus thing."

"Tell Gary, too."

"Alright," I said.

There were a few other kids hanging around but I didn't feel like trying to talk to them. I decided to get out of there.

Four

The host family lady let me in this time. She was a short, mean-looking woman with flabby arms, and she was even harder to understand than her son. She was working on dinner—the whole place smelled like burning flesh.

When I walked into my room my roommate Gary jumped up off his cot and gave me one of those crushing handshakes. He was a big tan guy with blonde hair sprouting out of his arms and legs. He was wearing a t-shirt that said COLORADO COLLEGE ULTIMATE.

"Hey!" he said. "I'm Gary."

"I'm Kevin."

"Nice to meet ya, Kevin."

"Likewise."

"What'd you do to your finger?"

"Broke it skating."

"Nice," he said. "Yeah, I saw your skateboard. Pretty cool."

"Thanks," I said. I didn't say anything about his Frisbee.

He was beaming at me. "Isn't this place great?"

"Yeah, it's cool," I said.

"You missed the big lunch."

"I know."

He nodded. "So you go to UC Davis, huh?"

"Yep."

"Cool. You must know Todd Becker."

Todd Becker was probably the biggest asshole at UCD. One of those student body president type frat boys who seemed to be everywhere all the time. It was pretty much impossible not to know who he was, even at a big school like Davis.

"Nope," I said.

"Huh." This only slowed him down for a second. Then he said, "So Mrs. Gasperi is a trip, huh? Out of a Fellini movie or something."

I nodded. We'd seen a Fellini movie in my Italian class. I think it was about clowns or the circus or something.

"You meet her son? Massimo?"

"Yeah."

"Isn't he hilarious? We gotta hang out with that guy."

"That could be cool."

"So what do you think of this neighborhood?"

"It's alright."

"I think it's awesome. It's like the *real* Italy, you know? I think we lucked out. Everyone else down by the Duomo is getting the cliché experience. We're getting the real deal."

"I guess so," I said. "But what's up with the building across the street?"

He turned and looked at the half-collapsed building. "Oh, I asked about that. Sr. Gasperi said there was a gas explosion."

"That makes me feel better."

"Oh, ha ha. Hey, I think we're gonna eat soon."

"Yeah, it smells rank."

He just laughed. "Oh, and they said the water heater is broken, but that it should get fixed next week."

"Oh, okay." So maybe that's what the son had been trying to tell me.

"Cold shower. It'll be good for you." He punched me in the arm and smiled. What the hell?

Gary really talked it up with Sr. Gasperi over dinner. His Italian was pretty good. I mostly just concentrated on not puking.

I thought all Italians were supposed to be good cooks. Not this lady. She'd served us cold noodles with some kind of paste squirted on top. Plus there was some grayish mystery meat on the side. I'm not a big health freak or anything, but I'm used to seeing something green on my plate.

The lady sat with us but she didn't eat. She just smoked and drank wine and didn't offer us any. She kept getting up to refill her glass from a bottle on the counter. We had the standard issue mineral water in greasy looking glasses. I asked Gary if he thought I could get some tap water.

"Why?"

"Cause this carbonated stuff is nasty."

"What are you talking about?" he said. "When in Rome."

"Yuck," I said.

"If you want tap water why don't you ask her?"

"My Italian sucks."

"This is your opportunity to learn. This is what it's all about."

"Whatever," I said.

So Gary asked her in Italian. She sneered, then said something I didn't understand.

"What she say?" I said.

"She said we should stick to bottled water. The tap water is bad."

"Great," I said.

After dinner I mentioned how Trish wanted us to meet them out in front of the Duomo at nine.

"She's pretty hot, huh? What's her story?"

"I don't know."

"Oh, come on. She said she knew you."

I shrugged.

Gary said, "I don't know man, I'm still kind of jet lagged. I'm thinking of reading a bit and turning in early."

"That's cool," I said. I was relieved. I was sick of going back and forth from downtown and didn't really want to deal with Trish or anyone she'd be hanging out with.

Gary read a guidebook for a while, then started writing in a large red book that said "My Journal." I asked him if it was really a journal and he said that it was—that he wanted to record all of his experiences in Italy. I thought about what I would write if I had a journal and couldn't think of anything I'd want to put down and save. I once had to keep a journal for an English class when I was in high school. I didn't know what to write so I just wrote some made up story about how I put my cat's tail down the garbage disposal. I guess my teacher didn't think it was funny cause he made me see the guidance counselor.

I was bored. Normally I'd just watch TV or something. I didn't really know what to do. I'd brought along the latest issues of Thrasher, which I'd already read twice on the plane. What the fuck, I guess I'd just read it again.

This issue had Tommy Guerrero on the cover. Looking through the article I got homesick. Tommy was from SF. He was my hero. I'd seen him skate once in Oakland and the dude had blown me away.

I flipped through and read all the ads. Then I read Skarfing Material, my favorite column by Chef-Boy-Am-I-Hungry. If you remember the scene in Rocky where he drinks all those raw eggs, that's kind of like a Chef-Boy-Am-I-Hungry recipe, except he'd maybe add something to the eggs first, like hot sauce and peanut butter. Each recipe was preceded by an existentialist rambling of some kind. Chef-Boy-Am-I-Hungry had a recipe for a Squid Eyeball Sandwich and Vito's Vittles. After the nasty dinner with Sr. Gasperi they both sounded pretty good.

I put away the Thrasher and got out my Walkman and listened to the Descendents "I Don't Want to Grow Up." It was an album I'd really liked in high school and I'd sort of re-discovered it over the summer. It seemed especially funny to be listening to it in Italy.

I started noticing that there were quite a few mosquitoes. We were keeping the balcony windows open cause it was so stuffy, and as it got dark the mosquitoes were just flowing in. After I'd swatted about ten of the little fuckers I said, "These mosquitoes coming after you, too?"

Gary looked up from his guidebook. "No. They must like you."

"I guess."

Gary went to sleep pretty early. I stayed up a bit more reading. My internal clock was all fucked up. I was tired but didn't feel like sleeping.

I wasn't too excited about having Gary for a roommate, but it could have been worse. My roommate freshman year had been this real quiet Indian dude who seemed bothered by everything I did. He was always asking me to turn down the music, and he got really bummed if me and my friends drank or smoked pot in the room. It got kind of stressful after a while. Gary was gung ho and annoying, but I could probably get used to it. Hopefully he'd give up trying to act like Mr. Positive around me all the time.

I could hear the TV still going down the hall, but otherwise it was pretty quiet. There didn't seem to be so many kids on mopeds in this part of town. No sounds that seemed especially Italian or anything. Smells maybe, but no sounds. After a while I shut off my light and fell asleep.

I don't know what time it was but I woke up with mosquitoes buzzing in my ears. I turned on the light. There were about fifteen mosquitoes poised on the wall over me—lined up like a squadron on an aircraft carrier. I think they'd been sucking my blood all night and were just resting, too fat to move. I swatted a few on them and saw my blood splatter across the wall.

I fell back asleep.

Five

The lady left out these hard little toast things—rationed, two each—along with some coffee that was all granular and nasty. Gary of course loved it—once again, it was the "real Italy."

Gary had taken a freezing bath before breakfast and talked about how invigorating it was. I couldn't face it again so I decided to just stay scummy. I put on a shirt that smelled like Aqua-Fresh.

When we got on the bus Gary immediately went to the back and punched his ticket. When I didn't punch mine, Gary said, "Aren't you going to punch your ticket?"

"I will as soon as I see an Italian do it."

So we watched. I didn't punch my ticket.

The whole crowd was at the center. It was about what you'd expect. There were probably thirty or forty kids from various colleges all standing around BSing. I don't know if it was Italy or what but people seemed kind of dressed up. I felt like a slob.

Those two chicks from the phone place were there. When they saw me they started giggling. One of them said, "I thought you were supposed to be Italian."

"Molto," I said.

They apparently knew Gary already and explained the whole thing to him. He thought it was pretty hilarious. He kept looking at me and shaking his head and laughing.

Then Trish sidled up to us. "Hi Gary."

"Hi Trish."

She got all pouty. "I thought you guys were going to meet us last night."

"Oh, yeah," Gary said. "We decided to hit the sack early."

"Too bad. We had fun."

"Oh yeah? What did you do?"

"Just walked around. The Duomo is so pretty at night."

"Oh yeah, I bet."

Then Arnie walked up. He was the other kid besides Trish that I knew from Davis. He was this nerdy guy from Sacramento who'd lived across the hall from me freshman year. The guy was kind of bossy and loud and had a way of saying inappropriate things. And he had this weird center part that reminded me of Alfalfa from The Little Rascals—all that was missing was the cowlick. Basically, I found him annoying and generally tried to avoid him. But he seemed to think we were friends.

"Arnie," I said.

"Kevin. How's it going?"

"Good," I said.

He wanted to shake hands, so we shook.

I said, "So, you just get here?"

"No, I've been here a few days. How about you?"

"Got here yesterday."

Then Arnie said, "Hi Trish." But Trish was talking to Gary and didn't even acknowledge him. Nice.

And that's when I saw Anne, the daughter of my dad's girlfriend. At first I didn't recognize her—she'd dyed her hair black and it looked like she'd gotten her nose pierced. But it was definitely her.

She saw me, too, and then we were both just kind of staring at each other. I was about to walk over to say hi when the director lady stood up front and started clearing her throat and told us to sit down. I grabbed the chair closest to me, between Arnie and Trish.

The director lady was an overly tan woman with a giant red sweater and lots of gold jewelry. She launched into a spiel about how this was the seventeenth year of this program, how they had assembled the best faculty yet, blah blah blah.

I glanced over at Anne. She was just sitting there, staring up at the director lady like everyone else. This whole situation was definitely a bit odd.

I guess I should back up a bit. First, about my dad: he was a shrink, and like most shrinks, he was a total asshole. According to my mom he was semi-normal when she first met him, but then he got mildly famous and started making money and the whole thing went to his head. When I was ten he bought a Porsche and wrecked it taking a freeway off ramp too fast. He had some discs fused in his neck and got addicted to painkillers. So he was already a dick, but after that he got to be an even bigger dick. My mom kicked him out.

My dad had dated a few women before meeting Anne's mom. None of his relationships had lasted very long and I wasn't expecting this one to last, either. The women he dated were mostly other shrinks he met at conferences. Anne's mom—her name was Cheryl—was a shrink, too. Just imagine the kind of weird passive-aggressive shit they could pull on each other. Anyway, after they'd been dating for a few months my dad decided he wanted me and my brother to meet Cheryl and Anne (he'd been telling me for months how smart Anne was, how she'd won all these academic awards), so he got us invited to her house Christmas afternoon for lunch. I was like, fuck...

I went over there with my brother, and when I got there my dad was in the middle of a marathon phone call with his crazy sister, so I was stuck with Cheryl in her huge kitchen, trying to make small talk while my brother fidgeted with a roll of Scotch tape. I remember that Cheryl wasn't wearing a bra, plus she was wearing this weird crochet sweater, so that freaked me out a bit.

Then Anne appeared. Apparently she'd had a huge fight with her mom before we came over. Cheryl made some condescending comment about how Anne had been "pouting" in her room. It did look like Anne had been crying or something—her face was a bit blotchy and red. I had barely said hi when my dad walked in all pissed cause the cordless phone battery had died on him. And then my brother, who had wrapped all of his fingers in Scotch tape, decided to try to cut them out with a pair of scissors. Somehow he managed to slice off the tip of his thumb, and we had to take him to the emergency room.

So that's how I met Anne.

The administrator lady was still blabbing away. I looked down at the schedule they had given us. It was either Renaissance History or Art History first thing in the morning (I'd signed up for Renaissance History), then the Italian classes, then lunch, then either political science or Dante in the afternoon (I'd opted for political science—some class called "Modern Italy"). There were a few events and field trips sprinkled throughout the calendar.

Then the director lady introduced each of the professors. The Renaissance history guy was a dork from the Midwest with a bow tie. The political science guy looked like he might be okay—he made some lame joke about Mussolini that I didn't get. Some nervous young guy with red hair and a red beard was teaching Dante. I was glad I hadn't signed up for that one. Art History was taught by a small, plump lady wearing all black and funny glasses. She looked kind of like Velma from Scooby Doo.

There were two Italian teachers—both real Italians. My Italian teacher (teaching the intermediate class) was a skinny older woman who looked like a total hardass. The lady teaching the advanced class was hugely pregnant and had a nasally voice.

I looked over at Anne again and saw that she was looking at me. She looked back down at her schedule and pretended to study it intently.

After all the profs had been introduced it was time for us all to "get to know each other." I guess they had decided that public humiliation was the best way to accomplish this, and so they staged a "talent show" where everyone had to get up and do something.

It took a while for them to find the first volunteer, but finally Arnie got up and recited some Dante in Italian. Good old Arnie. So anyway, that got things going.

Gary was the next—he spun a book on his finger like a Frisbee.

Trish sung "Amazing Grace."

One of the phone chicks was double jointed. Her elbow could bend way back. It was kind of disgusting, actually.

I'd been into breakdancing for a while when I was a kid. There wasn't any cardboard so I just did it on the cold marble floor. I tried to think of the old LL Cool J tune I used to do it to (You Can't Dance) and somehow made it through most of the moves without falling, though I goosed myself on my wallet (we had been told to carry our wallets in our front pocket to avoid pickpockets). Anyway, it got a pretty good reaction from people.

Anne went last. She stood up and held her breath. She slowly turned purple and one of the phone chicks said, "Oh my god." I wasn't sure what she was trying to prove by it but I thought it was pretty cool. She held her breath for a really long time. Toward the end I thought she was staring at me but I wasn't sure. She finally let her breath out and took a bow. A few people clapped.

There was a short break before we were supposed to go off to our respective Italian classes, so I finally got a chance to walk over to Anne.

"Hey," I said.

"Hey," she said. Then she said, "Nice break dancing."

"Hey thanks. You did a good job holding your breath."

"Thanks."

She was wearing tight black jeans and a black hooded sweatshirt with bleach stains on it. She had like fifty bracelets on one arm.

"So this is kind of weird," I said.

"Yeah," she said.

"How's your mom?" I said.

"Fine. How's your dad?"

I shrugged. "The same."

"Looking forward to their visit?"

Just before I left, my dad got invited to speak in Nice. I had been hoping that it would fall through or get cancelled.

I said, "I'm still hoping it's not going to happen."

"They just bought the tickets."

"Serious?"

"I talked to my mom yesterday."

"Shit."

"So when are they coming?" I said.

"During the last week."

"Oh," I said. "That's good. We have some time to figure out how to not be here."

"Yeah," she said. "We need to start working on that."

Neither of us seemed to know what to say at that point. So I said, "So what level Italian are you in?" I said.

"Advanced."

"Figures," I said.

"Oh, whatever," she said. "What about you?"

"I'm with the dumbshits."

And then they were calling us to go to our respective Italian classes.

"See you around," she said.

"Yep."

The intermediate class was pretty big, so I was hoping to just kind of fade into the back. But the teacher immediately made us all stand up and tell people where we were from—in Italian. When it was my turn I stood up and said, "Sono da California." A bunch of people laughed. Maybe cause my accent sucked so bad. Or maybe they were thinking about my break dancing.

And I was right about that teacher—she was a total hardass. I got called on a few times and fucked up just about every time. And every time she would make me say it over and over til I got it right. It sucked. At the end of class she handed out the books: "Ciao."

At lunch I purposefully sat by myself at a table in the corner, but then Gary came over and was followed by all the phone chicks.

The blonde phone chick was named Wendy. The tall dark-haired one was Amy. Wendy asked me where I went to school.

"UC Davis," I said.

"Oh," she said. "That explains it."

"What is that supposed to mean?" I said.

She didn't answer.

Just then the advanced Italian class walked in, which was Anne, Arnie and four or five other people. They all sat down at an empty table across the room.

Trish said, "I guess that's the smart people table."

"They seem kind of full of themselves," Wendy said.

I glanced back over my shoulder. There was also this plump girl and two guys wearing matching cardigan sweaters who looked like twins. Anne caught me looking at her. She just kind of narrowed her eyes a bit and then looked away.

Everyone at our table started talking about their host families. Trish was really excited about her host family and house. Apparently her bedroom had fifteen foot high ceilings. Wendy and Amy were living with some artist lady who sounded pretty cool—she wore all black and was a Buddhist. Gary went on and on about our situation. It was like he was describing a totally different place. I didn't bother to insert my version.

The food was decent so I pretty much ignored people and focused on eating. It was basically a cafeteria with pasta and salad and stuff. Best of all they had normal tap water, served with little slices of lemon. I drank like five glasses.

Toward the end of lunch Gary started talking about how his dog was sick, and that he was probably going to be put to sleep in the next week, and that he was sad he couldn't be there.

Trish said, "Oh my god, that's so sad." She reached out and touched Gary's arm.

Six

After lunch there was a mass trip to some museum. We walked back over the Ponte Vecchio and then through the streets of Florence. It was like a little parade.

I hate museums. Plus everyone was walking so slow and I was sick of listening to all the stupid conversations. I decided to ditch out. I slowly drifted to the back of the group and then turned down an alleyway. No one seemed to notice.

I walked around for a while and then stopped and had another gelato. Then I walked back toward the Arno and started walking on this road that ran parallel to the river. That's when I ran into Anne. She was leaning on the wall, smoking and looking out at the water.

"Didn't feel like going to the museum?" I said.

"I've been looking forward to seeing Caravaggio in person for a long time. It would totally ruin it to look at it for the first time with a bunch of lame-os."

I didn't know who Caravaggio was but I said, "I know what you mean."

She turned and looked back down at the river. "Do you think you can walk out there?"

She pointed at this long cement dam-like thing that spanned across the river. There was water flowing over part of it but it looked like you could walk right out onto it from the shore.

"It looks like we could get down over there," I said. I pointed to a crumbling stairway about a hundred yards away which led down to the side of the river.

"Let's do it," she said.

We sat out on that dam in the middle of the river. We were surrounded by Florence but totally distanced from it all, too. The water was brown and dirty looking. If the river hadn't been flowing through Florence there would have been nothing special about it.

I didn't know what to say so I asked her how Reed was going.

"It sucks. I want to transfer to NYU but my mom won't let me."

"Why not?"

"She thinks I'll get in too much trouble there."

"That sucks."

"Yeah. My mom can be a total bitch." Then she said, "How's Davis?"

"It's alright."

"Do you know Arnie?"

"Yeah," I said.

"He's funny," she said.

"Yeah," I said.

I didn't really want to talk about Arnie, so I asked about the long scar I'd noticed on her arm. It was pink and livid under all the bracelets. She told me that in high school she flipped her mom's car. Her arm had gone through the glass and gotten wedged in between the door and a tree. She had no feeling in three fingers.

"Ouch," I said.

She shrugged. "Could have been worse," she said. "Actually, in a weird roundabout way it ended up meaning I got to spend the summer with my dad in Singapore, so that was cool."

"Cool," I said. I wanted to say, "What does your dad do?" but I hated it when people asked me that question, so I didn't say anything.

Anne had written all sorts of stuff on her Chuck Taylors with a magic marker. On one side it said, "Adam is a shit."

"Who's Adam?" I said.

"My ex-boyfriend."

"He's a shit?"

"Pretty much."

She'd also written "AC/DC."

"You like AC/DC?" I said.

"Not really. It's a joke."

"Yeah? What's the joke?"

She just looked at me.

"Oh," I said. "Okay."

I wondered if anyone had ever sat alongside the Arno and talked about AC/DC. Probably a few people.

Then she said, "So what did you do this summer?"

"Nothing," I said. "Sat around and watched TV." But then I told her about the whole breakup with Kate. I don't know why. Laying it out like that for the first time to a total stranger, I was able to see it for what it was—just kind of lame. I was surprised, actually. Over the last few weeks I had been thinking I still wasn't over it. But maybe I was?

Anyway, Anne seemed to understand. She said, "That sucks."

"Pretty much," I said.

"All relationships suck," she said.

"Yeah," I said. "No more for me."

"Me, too." Then she said, "Let's make a pact."

"Okay," I said.

She wanted to shake on it. So we shook. Her hand was small and kind of clammy.

I guess we were out there for a long time, because after a while we saw our group traipsing back to the center—just heads and backpacks above the wall alongside the river.

"There they go," Anne said.

"What a bunch of dorks."

Anne laughed. Then she said, "You can be kind of a jerk."

"What?" I said. "Sorry."

She laughed. "That's okay. It's funny."

I lay back. "So do you think we'll have to go to class and everything?"

"Yeah," she said. "What did you think?"

"I don't know. It just seems more serious than I thought it would be." Then I said, "You're probably happy."

"What is that supposed to mean?"

"Oh come on. My dad said you're one of those dean's list people. You probably get straight As without even trying."

"No," she said. But she was blushing and I knew it was true.

Then she said, "We should go."

Seven

I took the wrong bus home and got lost and took another bus and had to get off and buy a map and walk the rest of the way and when I finally got back it was late. I was tired and had a sunburn.

The lady started going off on me the second I walked through the door. I thought she was pissed at me for being late until she took me into our room and pointed at all the blood stains on the wall. I admit it did look pretty bad in the light—with these big brownish splatters all over the wall.

"Sorry," I said.

She yammered on about them for a while, then shook her head and walked out of the room.

Gary was just sitting on his cot, laughing. "Man, she really loves you."

"Whatever," I said.

"So where'd you disappear to? We were all wondering where you went."

"I don't know, just walked around a bit." Then I said, "So when's dinner? I'm starving."

"We already ate."

"What? Did she leave anything for me?"

"I don't think so. You wouldn't have wanted it anyway, it was pretty gross."

"Great."

"I have some granola bars if you want."

"No thanks."

I went out on the balcony and stared at the blown-up apartment building across the way. I couldn't believe I lived in this fucking dump with this psycho woman. Anne had said that her family was like the Italian version of the Cleavers and that it was freaking her out. She had offered to trade with me. I was starting to think I should take her up on that.

After a while Gary came out, too.

"You going out tonight?" I said.

"Nah. I want to study Italian a bit. Plus, I want to write in my journal about what we saw today. Those Caravaggio paintings were awesome."

A lone moped sped by below.

I said, "Maybe I'll take you up on that granola bar."

Eight

The next day we actually had to start going to class.

Renaissance History was super boring. I couldn't pay attention at all. I just can't bring myself to care about the Renaissance. I have a hard time caring about anything before the 20th century. Except maybe the Romans and the Incas and Sir Francis Drake and the Gold Rush and stuff like that. But I don't care about old paintings or a bunch of lame kings and popes. I was pretty sure that the teacher was wearing the same bow tie he had worn the day before. I wondered if it was a clip-on.

Next we had Italian class. I swear, the teacher had it out for me. She must have called on me ten times, and I screwed up most of them. And she would just stare at me as I floundered around. It was humiliating. I couldn't see how I was going to be able to handle it every day.

At lunch I ended up with Gary and the chicks again. I don't know how these patterns get established but they just do. I felt like I was in junior high again and I was at the popular table.

Amy and Wendy started talking about how the woman they were living with was totally insane. Apparently she was a serious Buddhist—not just some dilettante—and she spent most of her time chanting. Like, hours. She also had really loud and frequent sex with her boyfriend, which freaked them out. The whole thing sounded pretty hilarious to me.

Anne was still sitting over at the smart people table. I kind of wanted to go over and say hi but Arnie was sitting there and I didn't want to have to talk to him.

Anne was in my political science class, though. I didn't end up sitting next to her cause she was sitting next to that chubby girl from the smart people table. And anyway I had walked in with Trish and the phone chicks (Gary was taking Dante so I guess he was in there with Arnie). Plus Anne looked pretty serious about being in class—she had a pen and notebook out, all ready to take notes.

Political science was fairly interesting, actually. People make fun of the Italian system of government but it's kind of cool. There are like a million different parties so it's pretty easy to find one you'd actually want to vote for, unlike in the U.S. where you just have the same old two lame choices. And the teacher was pretty cool, too. He seemed to know a lot about what he was talking about, but he also seemed really relaxed and acted like he found the whole topic pretty comical, which was nice. Still, it's hard to pay attention after a huge Italian-style lunch, and I was fading fast by the end of the lecture.

I talked to Anne a bit after class. She was acting kind of weird—like I was bugging her or something (and maybe I was). Also, her nose piercing had gotten infected—it was all swollen and it was hard not to stare at it while talking to her.

I needed to call my mom. It turned out she had called the apartment the first day but the lady didn't give me the message—she gave it to Gary who forgot to tell me for two days. So I walked over to the phone place after Italian class.

I was dreading talking to my mom because I knew I'd have to pretend like I was having a great time. I hated that. But no one answered when I called so I was off the hook. I left a message.

I finally found this mini supermarket type place so I went in and bought a warm Coke (if you buy a cold Coke at a café or ice-cream stand they're like three bucks). It was 33cl which is just a bit smaller than 12 oz, but when I drank it I felt like I was missing that last ounce.

I was really starting to crave a tall glass of milk. The milk they sold in Italy was nasty whole milk. And it wasn't your regular whole milk, it was this weird stuff that came warm in boxes.

I also bought toothpaste. They didn't have Aqua-Fresh. They had Italian Colgate but I never really liked Colgate so I picked out some weird Italian stuff called Pasta del Capitano. Gusto Fresco! Whatever that meant. But I liked the old school picture of the dude with a mustache. Maybe he was the captain.

After that I decided I should go back to the apartment. We already had a serious amount of reading. That just seemed wrong somehow. I was over here in Italy and I was supposed to spend all my time reading?

Nine

Friday was pretty much like Thursday, only I was already getting seriously behind on the reading. But then it was the weekend so I didn't care.

That night Gary and I met the chicks at this club called the KGB bar. Wendy and Amy had heard about the place from these Eurotrash guys who had picked them up at a gelato stand. The Eurotrash guys met us all down there. They had greasy hair and goofy looking shirts and seemed a bit bummed to see me and Gary. Still, they made a big effort to kiss our ass, and their English was hilarious. When I told them I was from California they asked me if I'd met Harrison Ford.

The Eurotrash guys danced with Wendy and Amy, and Gary danced with Trish. I sat in the corner and drank. I wanted to drink beer but beer is really expensive in Italy, so I drank wine, which is kind of gross to drink in any kind of quantity.

The place was kind of cool though, cause it was filled with Moroccans and Africans. It was a nice change from cheesy Italians and dumb Americans.

Afterwards the Eurotrash wanted to take Wendy and Amy somewhere and Trish and Gary were kind of hesitating like they just wanted to go off by themselves. I decided to get out of there.

I went to the bus stop. I waited around for a while before I figured out that I'd missed the last bus. So then I just popped Zen Arcade into my walkman and walked home.

The streets get totally empty once you get out of Centro. If I had been in the US I would have been worried about being mugged. I'm sure there are muggers in Italy but it seemed sort of comical so I didn't worry about it.

I'd forgotten my key so I hit the buzzer and woke everyone up. The son seemed bummed. He was wearing a shirt that said "Indiana Jones" so that was the second Harrison Ford reference in just a few hours.

I went out and sat on the balcony. In a weird way I was actually getting used to this. I mean, everything was so lame that it was actually kind of funny. I wondered what Anne had done that night. Probably nothing. I'd talked to her for a second in political science earlier that day. She was acting a bit more normal but her nose had seemed even more infected.

Gary came in two hours later and woke everyone up again which made me smile.

Ten

My main goals for Saturday were to do my laundry and to skate. Sr. Gasperi had offered to do our laundry for us but apparently we were supposed to pay her. Gary seemed fine with this but it just seemed wrong to me. Plus, I didn't like the idea of her touching my boxer shorts.

Thing is, I wasn't clear on whether we were allowed to use the washing machine on our own or not. I would have gotten Gary to ask, but he'd gotten up early to go meet Trish somewhere. Plus I think he was getting sick of translating for me all the time. I went to try to ask Sr. Gasperi myself but as far as I could tell she wasn't around. So I decided to just go for it.

The washing machine was in the bathroom. It was really small—it looked more like a microwave. But somehow I managed to shove in most of my clothes. I found some stuff that looked like detergent and poured it into the little slot in the side. Then I hit the button. A light came on but nothing happened. I looked around, made sure it was plugged in and everything was connected, then tried again. Still, nothing.

I finally figured out that the water hookups weren't turned on. When I switched them on the washer started to fill up. I watched the water rise to the top of the glass window. Then it started turning around and around.

I went back to the kitchen to get some coffee. There was the standard ration of toast cracker things and a cold pot of coffee. I poured the cold coffee out, rinsed out the pot, packed in some new coffee grounds, screwed it all together and put it back on the stove. I turned on the gas but there didn't seem to be a pilot so I had to search around for this wand thing I'd seen Sr. Gasperi use to light the gas. I found it and finally got it going—not before I'd stunk up the whole place with gas. I decided I'd better check on the laundry.

When I walked into the bathroom it was like that scene in the Brady Bunch where Bobby decided to do the laundry himself and the whole laundry room filled with suds— except you have to scale it down to an Italian sized washer. Basically there was a lot of sudsy water on the floor. I don't know what happened. Too much detergent or something.

I mopped up as best as I could with a few towels and then rinsed all my soapy clothes in the sink. Then I went and hung my stuff out on the balcony. All my clothes were kind of gray looking now, but at least they were clean, or cleaner. It seemed like I'd gotten most of the toothpaste out, too. So, I'd accomplished my goal for the day. I went and got all the towels I'd used to mop up the floor and hung them up to dry on the balcony, too.

Then I remembered my coffee. I went back to the kitchen to find that it had all boiled over and made a big burned mess all over the stove top. Oops. Again, I cleaned up everything the best I could. I decided I'd better get out of there before something else bad happened. I grabbed my skate and left.

I don't know why, but I headed downtown—habit I guess. But as it turns out, skating in Italy is one of the coolest feelings in the whole world. And for the first time in a while, I felt totally free.

People in California are pretty used to skaters, used to that sound. But Italians obviously hadn't seen or heard skaters much in Italy. People would stop and stare at me. And I had pretty hard wheels so it was pretty noisy.

Most of the surfaces weren't that bad, but the closer I got to downtown, the worse it got. At one point I thought my teeth were going to come out. Then I got to some really hardcore cobbles and just had to stop and walk.

I didn't feel like dealing with any tourist shit so I went and bought another warm Coke and some bread and went out and sat on that dam thing out in the middle of the Arno again.

I wondered what Anne was up to. I was starting to think she hated me. I'd seen the looks she'd given Trish and Wendy and Amy. She probably thought I was an idiot for hanging out with them, and I didn't blame her.

Nine more weeks of this. What the hell was I going to do? Living abroad was supposed to be one of those great life experiences but it just kind of sucked. I finished my Coke and bread and got up to walk around a bit. I didn't even bother trying to skate on most of the downtown streets.

I'd only been wandering around for about ten minutes when I saw Arnie. He was sitting at this café reading The Herald Tribune.

I wondered if he was as bored as I was. I wondered if he was having a shitty time, too. Who knows? He was probably having a great time. He probably loved it here.

Anyway, I don't think he saw me, so I kept walking.

I remembered that I wasn't going to get dinner at home that night so I decided to try to find something to eat on my own. I finally found a pizza place that looked ok. And they didn't seem to make a big deal out of my skateboard or anything, which I appreciated. I ordered pizza and wine and the waiter brought me a whole bottle of wine, which was cool.

The pizza arrived. It was super thin and barely had anything on it. I'd heard about that. But it wasn't too bad once you got used to it. It's just not like real pizza. Or real American pizza anyway.

I was feeling pretty suave until some other American students came in and started acting like total retards. This one guy with a Yankees cap kept being really loud and ordering the waiter around in English like he owned the place.

Man, Americans are stupid. Italians were weird and all but I was starting to see how dumb Americans were. Or maybe it was just the kinds of Americans who were tourists or went to study in other countries. Still, it was embarrassing.

I finished my pizza and got out of there.

I had been thinking I should try to wait around a bit more and then try calling my mom again, but I didn't feel like being downtown anymore and having to dodge other Americans students and tourists and kids on scooters. And I had the feeling that if I did call I'd probably just end up getting my stupid brother again. So I decided to skate on back to Baltimore. Maybe do some homework. Or not.

It was getting dark and the streets were pretty empty. The sidewalks smoothed out after a bit and I really flew.

Eleven

The Eurotrash dudes had given us some hash the night before. It was basically this little pasty block of brown stuff that looked kind of like clay. To smoke it you had to break off little bits and then roll the bits into a cigarette. I'd been a pot smoker since I was like twelve but had never smoked hash, and I'd never smoked cigarettes, 'cept for maybe one or two menthol Benson & Hedges that Kate used to smoke. Anyway, Gary and I rolled the hash into a Camel we'd bummed off the Eurotrash dudes and smoked it out on the balcony.

"This shit is weak," I said.

"Yep," Gary said, coughing. He handed me the cigarette and picked up his Frisbee. He was always messing with his Frisbee—spinning it and doing stupid tricks. It was like a nervous tick with him. It was starting to bug me.

"Let me see that," I said.

He threw it to me. We started tossing it back and forth. I'm not that great with Frisbees. I never really got into the whole Frisbee thing. Eventually I made a lame throw and it sailed off the balcony.

"Nice one," Gary said. "Go get it."

"You go get it."

"Ha. You threw it."

"You missed it," I said.

Gary just said, "Dude."

"Alright," I said. "Just let me back in."

It had seemed obvious where the Frisbee had gone from above, but once I was down at street level I couldn't see it. I looked up for Gary but I couldn't see him.

"Gary!" I said.

A dog was barking somewhere. I was starting to feel somewhat stoned. Maybe the hash was working after all.

I went and looked around some parked cars. Two guys were walking by. Their leather shoes made scuffing noises on the sidewalk. They stopped and said something to me that I didn't understand.

"Non capisco," I said.

They said something else and then shook their heads and kept walking.

I heard Gary yell, "Find it?"

I looked up at our building but couldn't see where Gary was. "No," I said.

"It's over there!"

I finally spotted Gary. I had been looking at the wrong building. Man I was turned around.

"Where?" I yelled.

"It went over there!" He was pointing somewhere behind me. I turned around to look but all I saw was this brick wall.

When I looked back at Gary I saw that some old lady had walked out onto the balcony below ours. So now I had an audience.

"I can't find it," I said.

"Come back and let me try," Gary said.

Gary buzzed me back in and I went upstairs and he went down to look for the Frisbee.

About ten minutes later Gary hit the buzzer and I buzzed him back in. When he got back up I said, "Where was it?"

"Under a car."

"Oh," I said. "Sorry man."

He shrugged. "Don't worry about it." He went and lay down on his bed. I couldn't tell if he was pissed at me or what.

I said, "You feel stoned?"

"I don't know. I think I'm just tired."

"Me, too."

Twelve

I slept in on Sunday. Way in. Gary got up early to go to church, which kind of freaked me out. He must have gotten up at six in the morning. I was totally disoriented and asked him what he was doing like five times before I finally got it. Church. Not school or a field trip or anything, just church.

The whole religion thing was one of the weirdest things about college. All of a sudden I was around all these people who were serious Christians. It wasn't something that would come up right away, but it always came up eventually—at dinner, during late night conversations in the hallway, etc. I didn't get it. It seemed like the kind of thing you might play along with for a while to make your parents happy, but I couldn't see why anyone would take that shit seriously or waste any time with it once they had moved away from home.

When I finally got up I didn't know what to do. Because it was Sunday everything would be closed, not that I wanted to go shopping or anything like that. I was sick of "centro." But what to do? Just sit around the apartment I guess.

As far as I could tell there hadn't been any fallout from the laundry and coffee disasters the day before. The mosquitoes seemed to have settled down a bit, too, so that was good.

I had plenty of reading to do but didn't feel like it. I tried reading some political science but got bored. The Renaissance History reading looked totally lame so I didn't even bother. Something about lesbian nuns. The history dweeb had gotten pretty excited about it. Whatever.

I went out to the balcony to check on my laundry. Everything was dry now but kind of stiff. One of my socks had fallen down to the balcony below.

When Gary came back he didn't say anything. He just walked in and lay down face first on his bed.

"How was church?"

"Fine."

He didn't seem fine. "You okay?" I said.

"My dog died."

"Oh, shit, I'm sorry."

He didn't say anything.

We'd had a dog for like a week when I was a kid but my dad was allergic so we had to get rid of it. My mom bought us a parakeet to make up for it but we all thought it was kind of annoying and ended up getting rid of it, too. That was it for my family and pets.

Later on Massimo came into our room. He said a bunch of shit I didn't get. I was worried he was talking about the washing machine incident. Gary rolled over and looked at me.

"He needs help getting a TV out of his car. Can you help him? I'm too out of it."

"Sure," I said. I was kind of glad to have the opportunity to get back on everybody's good side. Massimo looked slightly disappointed when he saw it was me who was helping him.

I followed him down the street to his car, which was one of those tiny Fiats. Sr. Gasperi was waiting for us, smoking and looking glum. I guess she was guarding the large TV, which was wedged in the back of the hatchback.

I wasn't sure why they needed a third TV, and this one didn't look any better than the others they had. Whatever.

I was worried about my broken finger, so then of course I smashed the crap out of the index finger on my other hand as I helped to pull the TV out. Massimo just kind of looked at me blankly while I swore and shook my hand.

Getting it up the stairs was a total bitch because we had to walk sideways, plus I was taller than Massimo so I had to stoop over. And of course we had Sr. Gasperi behind us directing, which was distracting and annoying.

We were making our way up the last flight of stairs and I was leaning over and all of a sudden Massimo started talking really fast and the TV slipped through his hands and there was no way I could stop it. Crash! It didn't fall far, and the screen didn't break, but it definitely didn't sound too good. And when Massimo shifted it on the step we could hear a bunch of stuff rattling around inside the cabinet.

Sr. Gasperi was swearing a blue streak. I didn't know what to say. I went to help Massimo pick it up again but he didn't seem to want me to touch it. I guess all of a sudden Massimo had superhuman strength, because he was able to pick up the TV and carry it the rest of the way inside by himself. Sr. Gasperi shook her head and muttered something as she walked past me and into the apartment.

When I walked back into our room, Gary was still lying face down on the bed. He must have heard the whole thing but he didn't say anything. I lay on my bed, too.

Thirteen

"Dude, wake up."

...

"Wake up. We're going to be late."

I was dreaming about eating Mexican food—about biting into a big burrito with lots of guacamole and hot sauce. And I had a big glass of ice-cold milk. I couldn't decide which was better—the burrito with the guacamole and hot sauce or the tall, cold glass of milk. But then I opened my eyes and Gary was standing over me in our dark room and it was Monday and I was still in Baltimore, still in Italy. Shit.

Of course Gary was already dressed and ready to go. And of course Sr. Gasperi was hogging the bathroom. So it was another morning without a shower (the water heater was still broken, so it wasn't like I looked forward to cold baths or anything). And I couldn't even take a piss.

I don't know if Gary was still in a bad mood about his dog or what but at the bus stop he was acting all put out and irritated—he kept looking at his watch and then glaring at me accusingly.

Then on the bus he gave me a bunch more shit about not punching my ticket. When I didn't respond he started in on how I wasn't doing my homework.

"Did you do any reading this weekend?" he said.

"Some." I lied.

"Seriously, why did you even come here?"

"Good question."

In Renaissance history we had a lecture on this really crazy pope—Pope John the XIXXVVV or something like that. All their names are the same, but this one dude actually sounded kind of interesting. You think of popes as being kind of mellow and stuff, just wearing a funny hat and praying a lot and whatnot. But this guy was nuts. He killed like 10,000 people. And he didn't just kill them outright. He seemed to really be into torture, rape, incest, the works.

The history prof got all worked up about it during the lecture—he was doing this little dance as he talked—kind of jumping from side to side. I guess I could see why someone would be interested in some of this stuff, though it was funny that you could actually get paid for being interested in it. But I decided that maybe I should do the reading more often.

Italian class was pretty bad. I fucked up every time I was called on, and I kept slipping into Spanish by accident. The teacher was looking somewhat put out.

"Non e '*los*' bambini," she said. "E '*i*' bambini."

"Sorry," I said. "I meant i."

"Come?"

There was a bunch of snickering in the classroom.

"Yes," I said. "I mean si. It's 'i.' I bambini."

At lunch I got stuck listening to Wendy and Amy and Trish asking Gary about his dead dog. I couldn't tell if Gary was milking it or what, but the chicks were going overboard with the sympathy act. When I tried to change the topic to the weird-tasting potato dish they had served us for lunch (I think it's called gnocchi—you don't pronounce the G though), Trish got angry at me.

"His dog died. Doesn't that mean anything to you?"

"Yeah," I said.

"Yeah? What does 'yeah' mean?"

"Um, it means yeah. As in, yes."

Trish just shook her head.

After we'd said about everything you could say about the dead dog, Wendy and Amy started in on their favorite topic—the Buddhist. Apparently there'd been more clashes over the weekend. As far as I was concerned Wendy and Amy were acting like complete spoiled brats. And anyway, nothing seemed that bad to me after Sr. Gasperi. After a long harangue about hair in the sink I said, "She doesn't sound that bad."

"Well you don't have to live with her and hear the chanting and all that," Amy said.

"What's so bad about chanting?" I said.

"Oh my god," Wendy said.

"I bet you would chant with her," Trish said.

"I probably would," I said.

"Yeah," Trish said. "You seem like one of those guys who joins a cult, then becomes a mass murderer or something."

"What the hell?" I said.

"I'm just kidding," Trish said, laughing. They were all looking at me and laughing, even Gary.

"Ha, ha," I said.

Things got even stranger after lunch when I got called in to talk to the administrator. She was acting all agitated and weird. It took me a while to figure out that they had been calling around to check with all the host families to make sure things were going okay, and that Sr. Gasperi had complained about me. Apparently Sr. Gasperi had been especially angered about me brushing my teeth over the kitchen sink.

"She mentioned that?" I said. "Did she mention how she's always hogging the bathroom, and how there's no hot water?"

"No. But she did mention something about you dropping her son's TV."

"You've got to be kidding me. I was helping him move it. We both dropped it."

The lady just shrugged. "All I know is what she told me."

"What about Gary?"

"She didn't mention Gary."

"This is total bullshit."

Then I got a big lecture about how we were guests in their homes, etc.

"Look, why don't you move me somewhere else? Or maybe I can find a place. Seriously, I'd rather just get a cheap hotel or something."

The lady seemed pretty taken aback. She started shaking her head and mumbling about how they'd never had these kinds of problems before, etc. etc.

"Whatever," I said. "I'm late for class."

Political science started getting kind of dull again. The Italian political system had seemed kind of cool at first, but it just ended up meaning that no one could get anything done. The Communist party basically just made a lot of noise but never really did anything or got any power. Maybe Italy needed to get a crazy pope again.

I said this to Anne as we were walking out of class.

"You mean like Mussolini?" she said.

"No," I said.

"Then what?"

"I don't know."

Then she said, "So Arnie told me some stories about you yesterday."

"Oh yeah?" I said. "What did he say about me?"

"Oh, you know, just some stuff."

"Huh," I said. I wondered what Arnie would have told her. And then I was thinking... yesterday was the weekend. Anne was hanging out with Arnie on the weekend?

"What?" she said, somewhat accusingly.

"I didn't say anything," I said.

"What was that look?"

"What look?"

"That look you gave me."

"I didn't give you any look," I said.

"If you say so," she said. "See you later." And then she walked off.

I had to hang around downtown after Italian class so I could call my mom.

It was funny to think that my mom and brother were still sleeping, that their day hadn't even started. Mine was half-way over—I'd already been bitched out by my roommate, compared to a mass murderer by the chicks at lunch, scolded by the administrator lady, humiliated by the Italian teacher, and learned that the one girl I was even slightly interested was potentially being told all sorts of bullshit about me. I wished I was still sleeping peacefully in California.

At five I decided I'd waited long enough and called. My brother answered the phone after four rings.

"You woke me up," he said.

"Aren't you supposed to be in school?"

"I'm sick."

"Sure you're sick. Where's mom?"

"I don't know."

"You don't know? Could you look?"

"No."

"What do you mean, no?"

"Fuck any Italian chicks yet?"

I sighed.

My brother laughed. "I take it that's a no? Dude, what the hell's wrong with you?"

"Would you just get mom?"

"Fine."

My brother put the phone down loudly and disappeared. A minute later my mom came on.

"Hi honey!"

"Hi mom."

"Having fun?"

"I'm having a great time."

"I'm so glad." She asked me a bunch of questions about my living arrangements and the food and classes and I glossed over everything.

Then I said, "How are things at home?"

"Fine," my mom said. "Oh, I ran over a biker."

"A biker?"

"A cyclist."

"You ran over a cyclist?"

"I didn't run over him literally. Just bumped him a bit."

"Is he okay?"

"He's fine. Just a little scratched up. I need to buy him a new bike, though."

"When was this?"

"Saturday."

My mom was a pretty crappy driver. And she was always strangely unconcerned about all the havoc she created on the road.

"Well, I'm glad he's okay," I said.

"He'll be fine." Then she said, "Your father still planning to visit you?"

"As far as I know."

"Well, that will be nice," she said.

"Or not," I said.

She laughed. "You'll be fine." Just like the cyclist, I guess.

My mom and I talked a bit more, and I promised to call back again the next weekend. I told her to not run over anyone else. Then we hung up.

Fourteen

The next few days were just kind of lame. Gary was sick of me making him late, or almost late, so he stopped waiting for me in the morning. And without Gary to get me out of bed every morning, I started to let things slip a bit. First I skipped Renaissance History. Then I skipped Italian. Pretty soon I was rolling in just in time for lunch.

I still sat with Gary and the chicks at lunch but I didn't talk much and they mostly ignored me. Anne and I were still talking a bit every day after political science, with neither of us trying to make a big deal out of it. Her nose had healed so she was looking better again.

Back at Baltimore in the evenings I had dropped even the faintest pretense of trying to get along with Sr. Gasperi. As far as I was concerned she was just a stupid bitch. I don't care if she was old or Italian. I started bringing my Italian dictionary to the table so I could ask her about the food we were eating. We seemed to be eating a lot of beans and something she called beef but really didn't seem like beef. Seemed more like rat or dog or something. Gary didn't take part in these discussions. He seemed embarrassed.

I dropped in on the administrator lady to ask her if they had started looking into moving me. My question seemed to take her completely by surprise. I told her that I was giving Sr. Gasperi one more chance—that if we didn't have hot water or some decent food within a week I wanted out of the deal.

After school that day I tagged along with Wendy while she went to return some leather gloves. I think she'd had a fight with Amy or something, and Trish was going somewhere with Gary. Anyway, the gloves were diarrhea-colored and had little diamond-shaped holes all over them.

"What's wrong with them?" I said.

"Nothing. I just don't want them."

"Why did you buy them?"

"I don't know."

We walked down this street which was lined with expensive shops like Benetton and Gucci.

I kind of liked Wendy. She seemed like a ditz but she wasn't as uptight as Trish, and she wasn't quite as tacky as Amy. Still, I never knew what to say to her.

I said, "So how are you liking it here?"

"I love it," she said.

"Really?" I said. "You think you could stay here?"

"Maybe," she said. "I don't know."

"What do you miss most about home?"

"My Jeep."

The store where Wendy had bought the gloves was filled with other Americans. She went up to the counter with the gloves and her receipt.

I was watching a man and his wife looking at leather jackets. Their kid was standing over in the corner playing a Gameboy. I remembered how when my parents took us to France I brought this hand-held football game. I played that everywhere—in the Louvre, in the Pompidou, the Eiffel Tower, you name it.

Wendy was still waiting at the counter. She was kind of hot in a really conventional way. I decided I should just marry some nice girl like Wendy. Maybe even Wendy. We could go to Italy and shop for leather crap and drag our kid along.

I walked over and looked at some shoes for a while. They all looked really stupid. That's when I heard Wendy's voice rising.

"But I have the receipt!"

I looked over and saw Wendy waving the receipt around. This middle-aged Italian lady with a gold outfit was just shaking her head. Finally Wendy turned and stormed up to me.

"Let's go."

"What happened?"

"I hate Italy."

I followed her out of the store and down the sidewalk. When we walked by a trash can she stopped and threw the gloves in the trash.

"You sure you want to do that?" I said.

She just kept walking.

We went and got cappuccinos. Wendy calmed down a bit.

"I guess I could give those gloves to my mom."

"Yeah," I said.

"Or my sister."

"Yeah."

"No, I hate my sister."

"Oh."

We went back to the trash can but the gloves were gone.

"Shit," she said.

That night after dinner Massimo knocked on the door. Gary had gone out with Trish so I was just hanging out, reading my Thrasher for the twentieth time. I'd also smoked a fair amount of hash. I'd managed to get some more from the Eurotrash.

Massimo was wearing a T-shirt that said, "Fantasy Island" with a picture of that little dude in the white suit. He said something, then smiled and motioned for me to follow him down the hall. So I followed.

We walked into his room. It was the TV we had carried up the stairs. It was working perfectly.

"It's not broken!" I said.

"Si, si," he said. He was smiling.

"Right on," I said.

Then in English, he said, "You like, smoke...?"

"Uh," I said. I looked around. I was sure his mom was gonna come out of nowhere.

Massimo smiled and shook his head. He put his hands on one side of his cheek and pretended to be asleep.

"Oh," I said. "Cool." Then I said, "You want to smoke..?"

"Yes?" he said.

I still wasn't sure if he was offering, or if he wanted our hash. I guess he had smelled it when he came to our door.

"You have?" he said.

"Yeah," I said.

So then we went back to my room and smoked a bunch more hash.

Massimo was actually a pretty chill dude. He knew a little English—about as much English as I knew Italian—so we were able to talk a bit. But mostly we just smoked and laughed. At one point he tried to stand on my skateboard and totally fell on his ass. I was laughing so hard I almost peed my pants.

That was right when Gary got home. He just stood there and stared at us for a minute. "You sure this is a good idea?" he said.

"Sure," I said. "Why not?"

Massimo held out the hash cigarette.

"No thanks," he said.

Massimo shrugged. Then he shook my hand and walked out of the room.

"You're gonna get us kicked out of here," Gary said.

"Good," I said.

Fifteen

Friday we had a field trip to Siena so Gary made sure I got up on time. When we got to the center there was a big tour bus parked out front and everyone was just milling around. Most of the students had cameras dangling around their necks and half the chicks were wearing new leather jackets and had new leather bags. Basically a big mob of dorks.

I had to piss really bad. For some reason the center was locked up so I wandered off in search of a bathroom and ended up having to go in an alley behind this Fiat 500 painted like a big soccer ball. By the time I got back everyone was on the bus.

Wendy and Amy and Gary and Trish were in back. Anne was half-way back next to that chubby chick friend of hers. Arnie was sitting next to the red-haired Dante prof. I got one of the last seats, right up front behind the director lady and the annoying history teacher.

As we pulled out, the director lady started screwing around with the microphone, trying to get it to work. Eventually she gave up and decided to just stand up and yell back at everyone. Apparently it was going to be an hour drive, then we'd take a tour of Siena's Duomo (I guess every town had one), then they'd turn us loose for lunch and after that whoever wanted could meet up for a lecture on something or another.

It was kind of cool being up front and looking out that huge windshield. The driver was pretty hilarious. He was this skinny guy with a long nose and aviator glasses and a big gold watch that hung loosely on his arm. He drove like a maniac. The director kept asking him to slow down.

I'd ended up sitting next to this girl who I hadn't really paid much attention to before—this short stocky chick with really tan, muscular legs. They were almost orange. Her name was Dana and she was on a field hockey scholarship at Purdue. She seemed nice enough. We compared notes on our host families. I told her about the mystery meat and the cold shower and the bombed-out building. Her place sounded pretty generic—but in a good way. She said her host mom was a really good cook. Then I asked her questions about her huge Nikon camera. She was fairly serious about photography and told me about all the things in Florence she had taken photos of. She mentioned something about how her boyfriend was also into photography and had actually sold some of his photos to galleries. Then she reached into her duffle bag and got out some kind of moisture cream and started smearing it on her legs and arms. It smelled like coconut.

Behind us people were acting like total retards. Some guys were passing this chick's shoe around and she was hobbling up and down the aisle making pathetic attempts to get it back and saying, "You guys!" Gary was standing up in back spinning his Frisbee and someone was playing George Michael on a boom box. At one point this other chick got car sick (bus sick I guess) and puked into her hands. The driver pulled over to let her get off holding her puke out in front of her. They decided to just let us all off for a little break.

It was weird being on the side of the road in Italy. It was the first time I had been outside of Florence. It was just a road surrounded by fields. Could have been anywhere. Well, not really. The hills in the distance had that Italian postcard kind of look to them and the cars going by were all very small and Italian looking.

Anne and her chubby friend walked up to me and Dana. Anne was wearing a pink prom dress with combat boots.

"Having fun?" she said.

"Sure. You?"

She shrugged. "I guess."

The chubby friend seemed to be looking everywhere except at me. She looked back at the bus, then she looked at her feet. I noticed she was wearing these strange blue high-heeled boots.

"Is that kind of weird, puking in your hands?" I said.

"I don't know," Anne said. "Not really."

"I've never puked in my hands," I said.

"You haven't?" Anne said.

"No," I said. "I puked in a bag once."

"Paper or plastic?" Anne said.

Then Arnie walked up. "Hey," he said. He made a little wave to everyone.

"Hey," Anne said, waving back.

And that pretty much killed the conversation. I tend to enjoy brutally awkward social situations, but for some reason the fact that this one involved Arnie kind of put a damper on it for me.

Anne was studying Dana. Finally, she said, "You smell like a coconut."

"It's a skin conditioner," Dana said.

"Oh," Anne said.

The director started yelling at us to get back on the bus. The puking girl seemed better. Someone had given her some napkins and a bottle of water.

I kicked a smashed battery off the side of the road and into the weeds, then followed everyone back onto the bus.

Sixteen

Basically Siena was just a small version of Florence. They had this big square where they did horse racing and sold huge colorful flags. The place was full of Americans and Germans, plus two or three large packs of Japanese tourists.

The whole Italy theme park thing was starting to get kind of annoying. It's cool to be proud of your history and all, but the Italians really milk it for all its worth. Plus, everything they are so proud of happened like five hundred years ago. I know there are people in the U.S. who are into the Revolutionary War and the Civil War and stuff, but at least that is a bit more recent, plus it's not the main focus of interest everywhere you go, unless you are making a special effort to visit historic battlefields or places like that. But in Italy you can't go anywhere without a bunch of history being shoved down your throat.

The history prof led us into the Duomo and started telling us about everything. It was a lot like the one in Florence. I liked the way sounds bounced off the walls in these places and how the air felt really cool.

The lecture was really boring. Everyone else was acting really interested, though, so maybe it was just me. I felt kind of tired. I went and lay down on a bench for a while and stared at the ceiling. After a while they turned us loose for lunch.

I wasn't really sure who to hang out with. People were grouping up like we were back at the center at lunch. Dana had already disappeared somewhere—probably to take a bunch of photos. I walked over to my old gang to see what they were up to. Wendy and Amy were going shopping and Gary and Trish wanted to go find some lame sounding fresco for some paper Trish was writing.

"What paper?" I said.

Gary and Trish looked at each other.

"Oh, right," I said. "The paper. I already wrote mine."

Trish rolled her eyes.

Then Anne walked up and asked me if I wanted to go check out the bell tower, which was pretty freaking tall— it was supposed to be like five hundred steps.

I said, "Sure."

I didn't realize that Arnie and the chubby girl (I still didn't know her name) and the twins were coming, too.

The six of us walked across the big square and got in a line. We paid a few thousand lire and started climbing the steps. It was a pretty long climb. The twins had to keep ducking to keep from smashing their heads on the archways. Then when we got to the top Arnie didn't look so hot.

"You okay?" I said.

"Yeah," he said. He was pale.

"You sure?"

"I think maybe I'm scared of heights."

"I think you better sit down," Anne said.

"Yeah, okay."

After we got Arnie situated under an archway, the rest of us walked over to the edge and looked out. I admit it was a fucking killer view. You could see all the way out to Florence.

"Wow," Anne said.

"Yeah," I said.

We just stood there looking out. When I looked down I saw Wendy and Amy. I could tell it was them because Amy was wearing this retarded-looking neon green baseball cap.

"Hello little people," Anne said.

"Ever think how easy it would be to jump off?" I said.

They all just looked at me.

Anne said, "Do you mean that in a scary suicidal way?"

"No," I said.

"Oh," Anne said. "That's good." Then she said, "A friend of mine from Reed jumped off a building. I guess it makes a pretty big mess when you fall twenty stories."

There was a horrible silence.

Then the chubby chick said, "We should check on Arnie."

"Yeah," I said.

Arnie was doing better but didn't feel good enough to look at the view. We walked down very slowly.

Then we had to decide where to eat. I hate making decisions when you're in a group. It's not like I really cared one way or another, but everyone deliberating and making random suggestions and not making up their minds is lame. Anne wanted to buy food in a grocery store and go find some place to have a picnic, but no one had seen any grocery stores and there was no place with grass. Susan (that was the chubby girl's name) said she just wanted a cup of tea. The twins had no input. Then Arnie said he felt like having waffles.

"I don't think they have a House of Pancakes here," Anne said.

"They should," I said. "I bet they'd make a killing."

We finally ended up at some tourist place with Cinzano umbrellas that were filled with other Americans. I ordered a pizza off a picture menu with a bunch of photos that had turned blue.

When the pizza finally came it had a big green lake of olive oil in the middle.

"This doesn't look like the picture," I said.

"Quit complaining," Anne said.

Turns out Anne was a vegan. The salad she had ordered looked pretty nasty—all the leaves were brown.

"You should send that back," I said.

"It's fine," she said.

"I bet you'd send that back if we were in the U.S."

"Yes, well we're not."

"Come on, your Italian is good. You can bitch 'em out in Italian."

"Whatever."

Susan was sipping some tea and not saying anything.

"How's your tea?" I said, trying to make conversation.

She just shrugged. I don't think she liked me very much.

I ate my pizza and drank my small, watery Coke. I was trying not to drink it too fast, but before I knew it, I was done. I wanted to order another but they were like ten million lire.

When I finished I got up to ask where the bathroom was. I forgot how to ask in Italian so I just asked in English, which the busboy seemed to understand. He pointed me around the back.

The bathroom had one of those holes in the floor with these two textured spots for your feet. Of course there was piss all over the place and it smelled bad. I couldn't imagine having to take a crap on one of those.

When I got back to the table everyone was done and they had cleared the plates. But then we just sat around for a while, since no one seemed to know what to do.

Susan said, "Do you miss your friends?" I think this was the first thing she had ever said to me, and it sounded kind of aggressive. Maybe the tea had woken her up a bit.

I said, "What friends?"

"The Gary guy and those girls."

They were all looking at me now, even the twins.

"They're not my friends," I said. "I mean, they're friends but I don't really know them or anything."

"Oh," Susan said.

We wandered aimlessly after lunch. Anne seemed to be leading the way but she didn't seem to have anywhere in mind. She just turned down streets at random. Arnie had a map and he kept telling us what street we were on.

"Now we're on Via De blah blah blah."

Every once in a while someone would notice a door or window or shop they thought was cool and we'd all stop and stare at it for a while.

I felt vaguely ill. Why did the whole food thing have to be so complicated?

After a while we came to this little fountain that was empty. There was an overturned trash can nearby and this mangy-looking cat was poking around in the trash.

"Poor kitty," Anne said. She walked over and crouched down next to the cat.

"I wouldn't touch it if I was you," I said. "Probably has some weird disease or something."

She started petting the cat.

"Okay, go ahead," I said.

"We need to find him some food," Anne said.

Arnie said, "I saw a little store up that street. I could go see if they have something."

"That would be great."

I couldn't believe Anne was playing the chick card and Arnie was going along with it. It made me want to puke.

Arnie disappeared. After a few minutes he came back with a can of tuna.

"My hero," Anne said. She looked at me when she said this. "You don't care, do you?"

I shrugged. I didn't want to say anything, but it just seemed weird, interfering with a cat in Italy. Our whole being here seemed strange and artificial, and now we were feeding cats? If it was a cat in California we would have maybe taken it home or to the animal shelter, but this whole thing just seemed futile. Wasn't this the kind of shit Captain Kirk was always doing? He'd try to help some alien on some planet but at the end of the day he always had to go back to the Enterprise and the aliens he had tried to help would go back to their fucked lives, and so ultimately it didn't make any difference. I couldn't say any of this, of course. This is not the kind of shit you can say to chicks.

Anne basically ignored me after that and mostly talked to Arnie and Susan for the rest of the afternoon. Whatever. I didn't care. I tried talking to the twins but it was like talking to a wall, so I gave up.

Everyone ended up in their same seats on the way back so I ended up next to Dana again. Actually, I got the feeling she was expecting me to sit next to her. She told me she'd gotten lots of good photos.

"Cool," I said.

"What are you doing this weekend?" she said.

"Nothing," I said.

"Want to go out Saturday?"

"Sure."

"Call me," she said. She wrote her phone number on the inside of a film box.

"They let you use the phone?"

"Yeah, why?"

"The lady at our place hides the phone from us."

"What a Nazi."

"Yeah."

"So let's just meet somewhere."

"Okay," I said. I started wondering about this boyfriend of hers.

"Let's meet at the Duomo at six," she said.

"Can we meet somewhere else?" I said. "I'm sick of always meeting at the Duomo."

"Okay, where?"

I couldn't think of anywhere else.

Seventeen

I went downtown on Saturday to meet Dana. I almost decided to call and blow her off but I didn't want to deal with the phone and Sr. Gasperi and all that.

On the bus a bunch of guys were singing this goofy Italian song and laughing. That's one thing you'd never see in the United States: guys singing. Anyway, they seemed okay—they weren't the total Eurotrash Italian guys with the disco clothes and greasy hair. Plus, there was a cute Italian girl with them, and she smiled at me. One of the guys noticed her smile at me. He turned to me and said, "Americani?"

"Si," I said.

"Where are you from?"

"California."

"California! Bravo! I very much like California."

"You been there?" I said.

"No, no. I would like very much."

"You should go," I said.

"Maybe I visit you there," he said.

"Sure," I said. "Come visit."

"Yes, very good. Very good."

He said something to the others and they all nodded and smiled at me.

"You here for study?"

"Yes," I said.

"Very good time."

I wasn't sure if that was a question or not so I didn't say anything.

"You like Italy?"

"Yeah," I said.

"A little boring, no?"

"A little." I laughed.

"None è California," he said.

"No."

This got a lot of laughs from the others. One of them repeated, "Non è California."

"I am Antonio," he said.

"I'm Kevin."

"Very pleased to meet you."

He got up out of his seat to shake my hand. Just then the bus came to a stop and the rest of them all stood up to start getting off.

Antonio said, "Mister California, come with us."

I glanced out the window. It looked like we were just getting into the Centro area. I had two more stops to go.

"Little drink," Antonio said. He held his fingers together to show me that it would be very little.

"Alright," I said.

"Very good," Antonio said, smiling.

I followed Antonio and his friends off the bus and into one of those typical Italian cafés with the lame looking marble bar and lots of brass and mirrors and candy and cigarettes for sale and the TV going full blast.

Antonio winked at me. "Nice, eh?"

They all ordered some drinks and when they came Antonio handed me one. It was a thick, clear liquid in a miniature wine glass.

"Grappa," he said. "Very good. Try."

It was like drinking jet fuel. I must have made a face because they all laughed.

"You like?" Antonio said.

"It's okay," I said, coughing.

This made them laugh more. "Okay, yes. Another?"

"No thanks," I said. I looked at my watch. "I gotta go. I gotta meet someone."

"Beautiful woman?" Antonio said.

"Um," I said. "I guess."

He patted me on the back. "Okay. We are here. Come back later."

"Alright," I said.

The streets downtown curve all over the place, so it's hard to keep going in one straight line. Plus, I think I made a few wrong turns, so I was a bit late in getting to the Duomo.

Dana was all dressed up in a short skirt that showed off those beefy orange legs. She looked pretty good.

"You're late," she said.

"Sorry," I said.

"That's okay." She gave me a hug. She smelled like coconut.

The grappa was gnawing at my empty stomach. I said, "Have you had grappa before?"

"No."

"It's pretty nasty."

"So where do you want to go?" she said.

"Anywhere."

"Okay, let's go anywhere."

We started walking, and then Dana took my hand. She said, "I thought you might not show up."

"Why?"

"I don't know. I thought maybe you decided you didn't like me."

She kept holding my hand. I'd never been with a girl who liked holding hands. I felt kind of weird. And again I started wondering about that boyfriend she'd mentioned before.

We walked by a woman who was letting her tiny dog pee on the side of some five-hundred-year-old building. The piss zig zagged through the cobblestones.

"I don't get those," I said.

"What?"

"Those tiny fu fu dogs. I mean, why would you get a dog that could get its ass kicked by a cat?"

"That's so mean," she said. "What if I told you I had a Papyone?"

"What's a Papyone?"

"It's a tiny dog. His name is Penny and I miss him very much."

"Oh," I said.

And that's when we ran into Anne. She was by herself, walking toward us. I didn't see her until she was practically on top of us.

"Hi," she said.

"Hey," I said. We stopped but Anne walked past us without glancing back at us.

We started walking again.

"She's weird," Dana said.

Dana picked some place with a dirty orange awning. I managed to get a steak with some French fries. They didn't have ketchup, though. Still, it was pretty good.

Dana talked about her dog some more—I think to make me feel guilty about my fu fu dog comment—then she started talking about field hockey and how she was eating too much and getting out of shape.

I couldn't stop thinking about Anne. I wondered what she was doing. I was pretty sure Anne didn't have any stupid purebred dogs and I knew she would think field hockey was dumb.

After dinner we walked around some more. There's really nothing to do in Florence. I thought it would be cool to go sit out on that weird dam thing again, but Dana didn't seem like the kind of person who would be into it.

We ended up back at the Duomo again and were just kind of standing around awkwardly. I got the feeling she was interested in me but I felt tired and just wanted to go home.

So I said, "I feel like shit. I think I'm getting a cold or something."

Dana gave me a kiss.

"You'll get my germs," I said.

"I don't mind." She grabbed my hand again and said, "Let's go somewhere."

"Where?" I said.

"I don't know." Then she said, "I guess we could try going back to my place."

"Your place?" I said. "Are you sure?"

"Sure I'm sure."

"Alright," I said.

I followed her back to her place. She told me to wait outside while she checked things out.

She was gone for a long time. I was just standing there, watching as various Italians and a few tourists walked by. I was getting annoyed and I had to piss. I was just about to leave when she appeared again.

"Not happening?" I said.

"We just have to be really quiet."

"You sure about this?"

"You act like you don't want to," she said.

"Well..."

"Come on," she said, taking my hand.

I followed her up some stairs and through a large door and then down a dark hallway. I could hear a TV. It was kind of like my place but not as creepy and it didn't smell like burned meat.

We went into her room. She had a small cot like me. When we sat down the cot felt like it was going to collapse. We started kissing.

I really had to piss pretty badly. Finally I said, "I have to piss."

Dana didn't seem to care.

"Seriously."

She stopped. She seemed somewhat annoyed. "Okay, hold on a second. Let me check if anyone is out there."

She disappeared for a minute, then came back. "You can't right now."

"I'm seriously going to die."

"Ok, wait a second." She went out again and then came back with a San Pellegrino bottle. "Here, piss in this bottle."

"What?"

"Piss in the bottle."

"You're kidding."

"What? My brothers always used to do it on car trips."

"Car trips?" I said. "They pissed in San Pellegrino bottles on car trips?"

"Well, Gatorade bottles."

"There's a big difference between a Gatorade bottle and one of these."

"You said you had to go."

I thought I was going to lose it if I didn't piss. So I went in the corner and started pissing. It wasn't easy. Some was running down the sides, and then it seemed like I was getting near the top.

"Fuck fuck fuck…" I said.

Dana was laughing and I was laughing. Somehow I finished just before I got to the top.

"Everything come out okay?" she said, giggling.

You'd think that would have killed the mood, but Dana wasn't going to be put off any longer. The cot felt like it was going to give out. Dana was a really strong girl.

Afterwards she told me about her boyfriend who was on the swim team.

"He's going to kick your ass when he finds out."

"Great," I said.

She pinched me. "I'm just kidding!"

I didn't even care. I was really tired. I probably would have just fallen asleep if the cot hadn't been so small and uncomfortable.

I said, "I should go."

"You sure?"

"Yeah, I'm tired."

"Okay, let me make sure the coast is clear."

She re-adjusted her clothes and went back out there. I waited around for like ten minutes and she didn't come back. Fuck.

I tiptoed out of the room and spied around the corner of the kitchen and saw Dana talking to this Italian girl with a bow in her hair. It sounded like Dana's Italian was pretty good.

I got out of there.

It wasn't even that late. It was only like nine or something. I didn't want to go home and deal with Sr. Gasperi and Gary so I decided to go back to that café where Antonio and his buddies from the bus were hanging out. Somehow I found the place, and they were all still there, drinking and watching some weird game show type thing on TV.

Everyone seemed very excited to see me. I got hugs and pats on the back from a bunch of people I'd seen on the bus, and then more hugs and pats on the back from people I hadn't seen before. Then people started buying me drinks. I ended up drinking about five more

Grappas. It was easier now that I at least had some food in my stomach.

Antonio and his friends all seemed pretty cool. As far as I could tell they were all in their early twenties. They all wanted to know about California but I didn't really know what to tell them. Plus my Italian sucked so Antonio had to translate everything I said.

So then I tried asking a few people what they did and where they lived, which was a big source of amusement. Seemed that most of them lived at home with their parents and none of them really had full time jobs or went to school. They were just into hanging out and bullshitting, which seemed cool to me.

I gave up asking stupid questions after that, and kind of lost track of the conversation. It was fun enough just listening to the sounds of everyone's voices and watching their faces. From time to time something would make everyone burst out laughing, and Antonio would try to translate for me, but it was still really hard to understand. There was one story involving an umbrella that everyone seemed to find particularly hilarious. Antonio tried to explain it like five times but then he gave up.

And then I started thinking about Dana, but that made me depressed so I thought about Anne, which made me more depressed.

I guess Antonio noticed. He said, "Are you sad?"

I shrugged.

"A girl?"

I shrugged again.

"It is hard, yes?"

"Yes," I said.

He nodded. "Yes. Very hard."

It was funny cause right then I didn't feel any more alone or separate from people than I usually did. In some ways I felt even more at home with this strange group of Italians than I did with some of my oldest friends back in California. Or maybe I was just drunk. Anyway, I was bummed about how I had fucked up everything with Anne, but I was happy that I'd found some people to hang out with.

Finally I decided I better get out of there. I threw up on the way to the bus stop. Grappa is pretty rank.

Eighteen

I was too hungover to get up early the next day. I missed Renaissance History and then I was late for Italian.

I really sucked in Italian. Every time I got called on, I fucked up. Then the teacher asked me to wait after class so she could speak to me.

Someone said, "Busted."

Once everyone left the room, the Italian teacher said, "Did you take the required units before enrolling in this program?"

"Yeah," I said. "I mean, 'si.'" I was confused. It was the first time I had heard her speak English.

"Yes? Because it seems like you don't know any Italian."

I shrugged. "I know some."

"You need to work harder."

"Okay," I said. "I'll try."

She didn't seem convinced. She said, "Yes, please do."

That seemed to be the end of the conversation.

I hated it when people acted like they cared more about my education than I did. It seemed to happen to me a lot.

At lunch Dana came over and sat with me. She was

wearing this weird denim outfit. Wendy and Amy just kind of stared at her for a second but then went on with their conversation about handbags.

The chicks were crazy about handbags. I think Wendy had bought like five since we got to Florence. She was showing Amy a particularly ugly looking green one she had purchased over the weekend.

When there was a slight pause in the conversation, Dana said, "I found these really cute Prada knockoffs at a stall down by the Uffizi."

Again the girls just kind of stared at her. Then Wendy said, "Do you think that's okay, supporting thieves?"

"What do you mean?" Dana said.

"I mean these people rip off designers."

Dana's orange face was turning red. "I never really thought about it."

"Yes, well most people don't," Wendy said.

"What's Prada?" I said.

Wendy rolled her eyes.

Then Gary and Trish joined us. Trish said, "We got the tickets!"

Amy let out a whoop and clapped her hands together.

"What tickets?" I said.

"We're going to Amsterdam this weekend," Amy said.

"To see U2," Trish said.

"Oh yeah?" I said.

"They sold out like a month ago," Gary said. "We just found out that Mateo could get some." Mateo was one of the Eurotrash guys. Gary looked kind of guilty. It was pretty clear. I was being excluded.

Then Gary said, "Sorry."

"Don't worry about it," I said. "I fucking hate U2."

"I told you he'd say something like that," Trish said.

"Seriously? You don't like U2?" Gary said.

"Seriously." Then I said, "How are you guys getting there?" I said.

"We're taking an all-night train. It's like eighteen hours or something," Trish said.

Dana said, "I saw them at Red Rocks. It was incredible."

"It's going to be awesome," Trish said.

I really did hate U2. It was mostly because of Kate, though. Kate loved U2, and she'd had an Unforgettable Fire poster in her bedroom all through high school. The first thing I remember looking at after losing my virginity was Bono. She managed to drag me to one of the shows, and I'd nearly gagged to death from Bono's sanctimonious bullshit.

Still, I couldn't help feeling kind of bummed in political science. Amsterdam seemed like it might be kind of cool, and I admit I felt vaguely left out. Gary hadn't mentioned anything about it over the weekend. I guess I had barely seen the guy.

Out of habit I sat next to Anne but then I didn't know what to say to her, and she didn't seem inclined to talk to me. She probably thought I was a loser after seeing me with Dana. And she was probably right.

Dana found me after political science.

"You wanna do something tonight?"

"I have to study."

"Oh, okay."

"Sorry."

"That's okay. Maybe later?"

"Yeah," I said.

"Okay," she said. And walked off.

I wasn't very good at breaking up with people. In fact, I had no experience with it at all, except with Kate, and that had been a slow grind. I guess Dana and I weren't really together, or whatever. I don't know. I was an idiot.

Nineteen

That night I was sitting on my cot, sipping from the bottle of warm, flat water that I kept stashed in the room. We'd had another disgusting meal with Sr. Gasperi. I was burping up something weird. It tasted kind of like fish but as far as I could tell we hadn't eaten any fish.

Gary was doing his reading for Art History. Neither of us had brought up the whole Amsterdam/U2 thing since lunch. But I guess Gary was thinking about it because after a while he put his book down and said, "You seriously don't like U2?"

"I love U2," I said. "The Edge rocks."

"Whatever," Gary said. He looked like he was about to say something, but then he shook his head and said, "Never mind."

"What?"

"Nothing."

"No, what?"

"So what's up with you and that Dana chick?"

"None of your business."

Gary sighed and went back to reading his book.

"How's the book?" I said.

"Why would you care?"

"I don't know. Just curious."

Gary put his book down again. "Seriously, why did you even come here?"

"Why do you keep asking me that?"

"Don't you think it's a valid question? I mean, I assume your parents are paying for this. And you're just wasting everything, just wasting this opportunity."

"Wow," I said. "That's heavy, man."

"I'm serious."

"Now I feel all bad and stuff."

"Whatever." Gary started reading his book again.

I have to admit, Gary had hit a bit too close to home with his comments, and it pissed me off. My dad was always getting on my ass about "missed opportunities" and "making the most of things" and shit like that. But making the most of things generally seemed to mean memorizing a bunch of useless shit you'd never use again, or trying to be friendly with people you didn't like. Fuck that. And then you were supposed to be super grateful for everything, too. Yes, I wouldn't be here if my parents couldn't afford to pay for it. But did that mean I had to love every second of it?

Shit. Maybe Gary was right. Maybe I was just a spoiled ass.

I tried listening to the Descendents but somehow it just made me feel worse. So then I grabbed my skate and headed out.

The neighborhood really shut down at night. There was no one around and all the windows were dark.

For a while I just cruised from street to street. Then I found some steps to fuck around on a bit. It was a pretty cool spot. At home the edges of these steps would have been covered with aluminum residue, worn down and chipped by hundreds of grinds. But not here. I was feeling pretty good, doing Ollies and kickflips and stuff like that. See, I was making the most of my time here. How many people could say they had skated in Italy? And then, just as I was feeling really in the groove I came down wrong and twisted my ankle. Fuck.

I sat down on the steps and massaged my ankle. I was going to get arthritis when I was thirty. I wondered what I'd be doing when I was thirty. It was hard to imagine.

I looked at my finger. The doctor had said to leave the brace on for six weeks, but it didn't hurt anymore and it wasn't swollen or anything. It did stink and itch, though, and I was tired of having to hold a pen all goofy. So I took off the brace. My finger was stiff, but I could move it a bit. All better. I shoved the brace in my back pocket and skated home.

Twenty

The next day I was riding the bus to the center when I heard a bunch of commotion. We had just come to a stop, and all of a sudden the old ladies at the front of the bus started yelling and shoving. When I looked up I saw some dude wearing an official-looking uniform. He had a yellow booklet out and seemed to be checking people's tickets. Holy shit! It was a ticket inspector! So far I had only heard about these people but hadn't met anyone who had actually seen one. I was pretty far from the ticket machine and wasn't sure I even had a ticket I could punch anyway.

I saw that the back door was open, and several women were making a quick escape. I followed. A few seconds later the bus drove off and I was left on the sidewalk with two women who were having an animated discussion about the ticket inspector. I listened for a bit, then decided I might as well start walking.

I thought I knew where I was but pretty soon I was lost. I wasn't in the Baltimore area anymore, but I didn't seem to be anywhere near downtown, either. I couldn't even tell if I was going in the right direction.

One of my Vans had developed this farting noise and

it farted with each step. Of course it was the only pair of shoes I'd brought with me.

The sky was gray and it was kind of cold. I looked at my watch. It didn't look like I was even going to make lunch at this point.

I was still walking when one of those little Ape things pulled up alongside me and started honking its pathetic horn. If you've never seen an Ape, try to picture what would happen if a pickup truck had sex with a Vespa. It's basically a three-wheel scooter truck thing. Anyway, I was about to flip the guy off when I saw that it was the dude from the chrome bar.

"Kevin!" he said.

I said, "Ciao." I couldn't remember his name.

"It's Antonio!"

"Right," I said. "Antonio. How's it going?"

"What you doing?"

"Trying to get downtown. I think I'm lost."

"Ah! I take you." He pushed the flimsy door open.

"Yeah? Okay, thanks." I slid onto the bench seat.

"Not a Cadillac, eh?"

"No," I said.

"Ha, ha, yes."

I looked around for a seat belt but didn't see one. He twisted the throttle and we were off.

Riding in an Ape is just what you'd expect. Kind of like being on a scooter with a bench seat. It was pretty rough over cobblestones. There was also a pretty bad exhaust smell.

"Dude, I think you have an exhaust leak."

"What?"

"You have an exhaust leak."

"Che?"

"Nothing." I slid the window open.

After a while he said, "I need to make a little stop." He pulled over in front of a café and got out. "Come on," he said.

I got out and followed him around to the back of the Ape, which was filled with stacks of towels tied in string.

"You help me? Okay?"

"Uh, okay. But I gotta get to class."

"This just take one minute."

"Alright," I said.

He handed me two stacks of towels, then grabbed two more stacks himself. I followed him into the café.

We walked through the café, past some dude behind the counter reading a paper, and into a dark back room. We dumped off the clean towels and collected sacks of dirty ones. Then we carried them back to the Ape.

"So this is what you do?" I said.

"Do?" he said. "Oh, yes. My family. It is my family business."

"Oh," I said. "Cool." I tried to imagine working for my dad. Or my mom. It made me shudder a bit.

"Now, I take you to class."

"Thanks," I said.

From there Antonio drove me to the center. Wendy and Amy walked up as I was getting out of the Ape. Antonio immediately shut off the engine and jumped out looking very excited. I introduced them.

"Very pleased to meet you nice ladies," he said. "Molta bella."

I could see Wendy giving him a look over. She looked slightly skeptical, but vaguely interested, too. I didn't think he had enough gel in his hair for her, but who knows?

"Nice to meet you," Wendy said.

"Yes," Antonio said. "Very nice." Then he said, "Maybe you come by La Bellissima."

"What's La Bellissima?" I said.

"Where we go the other night. The bar."

"Oh, the bar. Right."

"Yes, you come by. You all come by."

"Alright," I said.

"Yes," Antonio said.

Wendy just kind of looked at me.

Amy said, "We're going to be late for lunch."

Gary and Trish were already at the table. Dana was at her old table. When she saw me she waved. I waved back. Then I think she said something to me but I couldn't hear over the general din of the lunch room, and then Wendy was asking me, "So where did you meet Antonio?"

"On the bus," I said.

"He seems nice," Wendy said.

"Yeah," I said.

"He's kind of cute," Amy said.

I glanced back over at Dana's table but she was talking to someone else.

Twenty-One

Dana ambushed me as I was leaving the center.

"Hi," she said, somewhat aggressively.

"Hi," I said.

"You okay?" she said.

"Yeah," I said. "Why?"

"I don't know. You just seem kind of different."

"I do?"

"Yeah."

"Oh."

Was she pissed that I didn't sit next to her at lunch? Or maybe she was still pissed about the whole handbag discussion at lunch the day before. Or something else?

"So...?" Dana said.

"So, what?"

"Can't you say anything?"

"Like what?"

"Like anything."

"What do you want me to say?"

Just then Gary and Trish walked out together. Gary stopped for a second to tie his shoes. Trish seemed to be making an effort to look anywhere except at us. Gary finished tying his shoes and they continued walking.

I didn't know what else to say, so I said, "Sorry."

"Don't be sorry," she said.

"Okay," I said.

Dana turned and walked away.

I wasn't really sure what had happened there but I had a feeling things were over between me and Dana. Or I hoped so, anyway.

I had almost no Lire left so I went to get some money changed at American Express. I had a big wad of traveler's checks that I hadn't done anything with yet.

I've always felt weird about spending my parents' money. They pretty much gave me whatever I needed for spending money when I was in school but it was like Monopoly money—it didn't seem real. I'd made some money over the summer bussing tables at this health food restaurant, but then wasted most of it on beer and pot and pizza and video games. So now I was back to my parents' money.

Where did the money come from? My mom's money came from the money she inherited from her dad, who had made his money in real estate. My dad's money came from talking to rich people about their problems. So my tuition was mostly paid for by messed-up rich people money and my living expenses were mostly covered by real estate money.

After I cashed the travelers checks for a billion Lire, I went to the chrome bar ("La Bellissima") to see if Antonio was around. There was just some old dude cleaning glasses behind the bar and a lady smoking and reading a newspaper. I ordered a Coke and stood around for a while. No one came in and nothing happened so I left.

Twenty-Two

In political science on Wednesday Anne was making drawings in her notebook during the lecture. At first I thought she was making notes, but then I saw it was just doodles, plus sketches of people. There was one of me. It didn't really look like me but I could tell it was supposed to be me. Like I was a cartoon character.

"Is that me?" I said.

"What do you think?"

"I don't know."

"You don't think it looks like you?" She held it so I could see better.

"I guess it does."

She looked at it again. "Hmmmm."

We hadn't really talked much since she'd seen me with Dana that night. I wondered what people were saying about me.

Then she said, "So are you going to U2 this weekend?"

"What?" I said. "No. Why?"

"I heard Trish and Gary talking about it."

"Oh, right," I said. "No, fuck U2. They suck."

"I don't think they're that bad."

"Don't tell me you're going," I said.

"No, I'm supposed to go see my cousin in Livorno on Saturday."

"Your cousin?"

"He's in the army. They have a base there."

"Oh. Sounds fun."

"Not really. I barely even know him but my mom won't shut up about it."

"So you taking the train or what?"

"Yeah, it's only like an hour. I'm just totally dreading it. I'm totally freaked out by the army and I'm not even sure I can find it. Susan was supposed to go with me, but now she's freaking about a paper she has due."

I said, "I'll go with you if you want."

"You will?"

"Sure."

"Okay," she said, a bit hesitant. "It won't be that thrilling or anything."

"I don't care. I think I just need to get out of here for a while."

"I know what you mean."

And just like that, things were looking up.

Twenty-Three

Gary and the others left for Amsterdam Thursday. So for the first time I got to have dinner alone with Sr. Gasperi. That was exciting. She served me some weird brown slop, then just stood against the counter, smoking and reading a magazine.

The slop looked gross but it wasn't that terrible—or anyway, it was a bit better than usual. I said, "Molto bene."

She put down the magazine and glared at me. Then she said something I didn't understand.

I said, "Che?"

She just shook her head and went back to her magazine.

Later that night I was sitting on my cot listening to the Circle Jerks when Massimo came in. I had the volume up kind of high, so maybe he had tried knocking first and I hadn't noticed. Anyway, I didn't notice him til he was standing in front of me, and I jumped. He was saying something but I couldn't hear him. I pulled off my headphones and he said something again but I still didn't understand. Then he said, "Gary?"

"He left," I said. "He went to Amsterdam."

He looked confused.

"Va a Amsterdam," I said.

"Ah."

Then he put his finger to his lips like he was smoking. I laughed. "Si, si," I said.

"Si?"

And then I realized he wasn't talking about Gary smoking up in Amsterdam. He wanted some hash.

"Oh, no," I said. "I don't have any."

"No?" he said.

"Smoked it all. Sorry." Actually, I still had some. But I wasn't feeling very sociable and I didn't feel like getting high.

"Ah," he said.

So then Massimo pointed to my headphones—like he wanted to try listening. I gave them to him, waited for him to get it over his weird hair, then hit play. He made a face, listened for maybe five seconds, then gave me back my headphones.

"You like it?"

"È okay," he said.

"Okay," I said.

"Okay," he said.

We both laughed. Now I was feeling kind of bad, but it was too late to admit I had some hash. And I didn't really see how we could hang out unless we were high. The whole language barrier was a pain in the ass, but then again we probably didn't have that much to talk about, anyway. I guess we could talk about how annoying his mom was. I always felt bad for guys with annoying moms. Annoying dads (like my dad) sucked, but annoying moms were worse. I don't know how he could stand to live here. But then I wasn't him.

Antonio didn't seem to know what else to say, so he just shrugged and said, "Ciao."

"Ciao," I said.

He walked out.

I put my walkman back on. The tape seemed to be slowing down. I needed new batteries.

Twenty-Four

There was an optional field trip to Fiesole on Friday, but I had decided not to go. But by early afternoon I was going nuts around the apartment. I decided to go downtown to kill some time, maybe call my mom.

My shoe fart had been getting worse. I was pretty sure other people could hear it. There appeared to be a hole on the side of my Vans. It was like walking on a whoopie cushion.

I went into a shoe store I had seen downtown. I didn't like any of the shoes—they were all very Italian looking. I just wanted some Nikes or something but all they had were the goofy looking blue tennis shoes that everyone seemed to wear. Either that or sandals and stuff. Plus, the sales dude made no effort to talk to me—he just stood over by the window, looking out at the street. The guy had a weird mustache like Salvador Dali. Fuck it. I left. I walked down the street with my shoe still farting.

I went to the phone place and called home. This time Don answered.

Don was my mom's current boyfriend. He had moved in shortly before I went to college. He was an ex-hippie turned real estate agent. I don't think he sold that many houses but whenever he did he'd take us all out to this crappy Chinese restaurant to celebrate. He was an alright guy, though all the turquoise jewelry kind of bugged me.

"Oh, hey, Kevin!" he said. "How's it going?"

"Good," I said.

"How's Italy?"

"I don't know. Pretty good I guess."

"That's great," he said. "In fact, I was just thinking about you."

"Oh yeah?"

"Yeah, I was just thinking, I wonder how Kevin is doing in Italy?"

"Oh," I said. "Cool." I wondered if he was stoned. Sometimes he toked up when my mom was out of the house. Pretty hilarious dude.

"So, you seeing all the sights?" he said.

"The what?"

"Sights. You know, like... I don't know. You been to Venice?"

"No," I said.

"Oh, you should definitely go. It's amazing."

"I'll put it on my list," I said. "So I guess mom is out?"

"Yeah," he said. "She went out. I'm not sure where."

"That's cool. Just tell her I called."

"Will do," he said.

"Okay, thanks."

"And hey, take care of yourself."

"Sure," I said. "You, too."

After that I decided to go back to that shoe store. I just needed to buy something. When I got there it was closed.

So then I pretty much had two choices: Antonio's bar, or back to the apartment. I decided to try Antonio's bar.

Antonio was there with all his buddies. He seemed excited to see me. "Oh, good, yes, perfect," he said.

"What?"

"You see, I was just talking about you."

"Really?" I said.

"Yes. I was saying, my friend, Kevin," he said. "He knows all the beautiful girls."

"Right."

"Yes, yes. Wendy and Amy, no?"

"What about them?"

"You need to call them."

"They're gone for the weekend."

"Oh no," he said. "That is very sad. Where did they go?"

"They went to see U2 up in Amsterdam I think."

"U2? Wow." He clapped his hands together.

"Yeah," I said. "It's exciting."

"Why you no go?"

I shrugged.

"Bono. He is very smart I think."

"Genius," I said.

"Yes, genius."

Then I said, "So how's business?"

"Business?"

"The towels."

"Ah yes, very good. Very clean."

"Cool," I said. "So you guys gonna expand your operation?"

"Expand?"

"Take over," I said. "World domination of the towel business."

"Ah," he said. "No. I don't think so."

"No?"

"No. We are happy." He laughed. "Don't want to work too much."

"Oh," I said. "Cool."

"Yes," he said. "I like it cool."

Twenty-Five

Saturday morning I met Anne at the train station. We bought tickets to Livorno and then got on this slick-looking train. It was silver and red and the seats looked like they belonged in a Ferrari. We sat facing each other next to a large window.

"Susan called me and said she decided she could go after all. Then she found out you were coming so she decided not to."

"What's up with her anyway?"

"She doesn't like you."

"Yeah, I know. But I mean she just seems kind of angry or something."

"You'd be angry too if you were a lesbian from Texas."

"Are you sure it's not that she's ugly and no one likes her?"

"That's not nice."

"Do you like her?"

"Sure. She's a bit annoying, but who isn't?"

"I just don't get the shoes."

"What shoes?"

"Those weird blue boots."

"Maybe they're comfortable. Don't be such an asshole."

"Sorry."

There was a jolt and the train started pulling away. I was facing backwards, which always felt kind of weird. I had to press myself back into the seat to keep from leaning forward.

Anne was wearing an old Army jacket with two pins—one peace, one anarchy.

"Are you trying to confuse people?" I said.

"What?"

"The pins. Aren't they contradictory?"

"Anarchy is peaceful," Anne said.

"It is?"

"Yes."

"Oh." Then I said, "Think they'll appreciate it on the base?"

"I don't really care."

"How about your cousin?"

"No idea. I don't really even know him. I vaguely remember splashing around in the wading pool when we were like five or something. I met him one other time in high school and thought he was gay."

We were rushing through the countryside—blowing through small train stations at like one-hundred miles an hour.

"You ever see that movie, *The American Friend*?" I said.

"No."

"It takes place in Germany or France or something and there's this cool scene where they kill this guy and then Dennis Hopper pushes the body off a train."

"And?"

"I don't know. I just thought of it."

"Is that what you thought Europe would be like? Like in the movies?"

"I don't know. Why? Did you?"

"I guess I thought it would be different. Or maybe I just thought that I would feel different when I was here."

"Like what?"

"I don't know. I guess I just feel kind of lame here. Before all I could think of was this trip, and now I just want to get back to my real life. Only, I don't have a real life."

"I know what you mean," I said. It was weird to hear someone say out loud what I'd been thinking for a while. It also made me realize I hadn't really talked to someone since coming here. Gary and the stupid chicks didn't count.

She looked at me, then looked out the window again. "I'm just sick of the whole school thing. I want to do something real, you know?"

"Like what?"

"I don't know. Bake bread. Drive an ambulance or something. Be useful."

"You'd want to be a paramedic?" I said. "Pull people out of car wrecks?"

"Sure."

"My friend's older brother did that. Turned into a total speed freak cause they make you do like eighteen-hour shifts."

"What do you want to do?" Anne said.

"I have no idea. Maybe be a janitor."

"You'd be a good janitor."

"Thanks."

"Listen to us," Anne said. "We're in Italy. Most people would kill to be here and we're talking about driving ambulances and being janitors."

"The janitor at my high school was pretty cool, actually. I used to buy pot from him. I think he was into kiddie porn, though."

"That's not good."

"No," I said.

"You're one of those weird people who liked high school, aren't you?" Anne said.

"What?" I said. "Not really. I don't know. It wasn't that bad."

"I hated it."

"Why?"

"I don't know. I was totally self-hating."

"Really? I thought you totally had your shit together. My dad said you won the state essay contest or something like that."

"Yeah," she said.

"What was your essay on?"

"I'm not telling."

"Oh come on."

"No."

"Fine."

I guess Anne was right—I actually kind of liked high school. I didn't like the classes or anything, but I liked my friends. I liked doing sports and shit like that. I acted like a rebel retard and went to punk shows and smoked a lot of pot and stuff, but it was all basically pretty fun. In comparison college had been a big letdown. I didn't meet anyone as cool as my old high school friends, and the classes sucked just as much if not more. I was glad that I had more freedom and it was nice not to have to deal with my dad, but otherwise it kind of sucked. And then there was the whole pressure of not knowing what to do next.

I felt sorry for people who hated high school. Seemed like they had missed out on something. But these were generally people like Anne, who were getting their shit together. Unlike me.

Some dude came and looked at our tickets. Of course we actually had tickets but these ticket guys still made me nervous.

After he was gone I said, "Maybe I could be a ticket inspector."

"I can't really picture you in the uniform."

"I guess you're right."

"Uniforms creep me out."

"It's going to be a creepy day for you."

"I know. Plus the whole war killing thing." She shuddered.

"Your cousin isn't killing anyone, is he? He just sits around on a base cleaning toilets, right?"

"I have no idea. But he signed on for the killing part."

I shrugged. "Hey, we pay for it with our tax dollars. We're just as accountable."

"Do you think so?"

I shrugged. "Do you think there's any difference between being a janitor at a school and being a janitor in the army?"

"Yes," she said. "I do."

"Why?"

She shrugged.

"Well, at least he has an excuse for being over here."

"I guess," Anne said.

"I mean, it seems more honorable than just coming over to shop."

"I wish I was better at shopping," Anne said.

"Yeah?"

"Yeah, I think that's my real problem. If I was a better consumer I'd probably feel a lot less conflicted."

"You're probably right," I said.

The train ride was only about forty-five minutes. The Livorno station was just this big slab of concrete with a long low building that was painted the same faded yellow you saw everywhere in Italy. We got off the train with a bunch of people who dispersed in every direction. The train pulled away and we were just standing there.

"Now what?" Anne said.

"You tell me."

"Should we get a cab?"

"Sure," I said.

We walked out front and got in a cab. It was almost too easy. Anne told the driver where to go and we were off.

Ten minutes later we pulled up at the gate to the base. We paid the driver and got out.

It was a little guard station. We walked up and Anne told the guy why we were there. It took me a second to realize that we were speaking English to an American guy. But from the way he looked at us we might as well still be foreigners. He asked for our names and we gave them.

"You're not on the list," he said.

"We're not? But he's expecting us."

"Hold on." He picked up a green phone and dialed. There was a brief conversation and then he hung up and looked at us.

"Sergeant Jameson left the base last night."

"What?" Anne said. "But I just talked to him."

"He's not due back until Wednesday."

"Are you sure?"

"That's what I've been told."

"I can't believe this," Anne said.

I was actually kind of relieved.

"So now what?" I said.

"I don't know. What should we do?"

I shrugged. "Go back to the station."

"I guess," Anne said.

Twenty-Six

We decided we might as well go to Pisa. From Livorno it was a ten minute train ride and then a five minute bus ride and then we were standing in front of the Leaning Tower.

"It looks just like in the photos," Anne said.

"Yeah," I said.

"But more fake."

I laughed. "Yeah."

She laughed. "Is that possible?"

"Sure," I said.

There was this big field of grass and the Leaning Tower and behind that another Duomo.

"Wanna go to the top?" I said.

"I heard you can't anymore."

"What?"

"Yeah."

"That sucks."

"Should we go check out the Duomo?" Anne said.

"If you want to."

"Not really, do you?"

"Nah," I said. "I'm pretty sick of Duomos. But I'm kind of hungry."

"What time is it?"

"I don't know."

We looked around.

"Everything is probably closed."

"Yeah," I said.

"What's that over there?" She pointed to a little tourist stand.

"Let's check it out."

We walked over to the stand and bought candy bars and crackers and bottled water and Anne got a leaning tower snow globe. Then we went and sat on the grass and ate.

There weren't that many people hanging around. Maybe tourist season was over.

After I finished my candy bar I lay back and looked up at the sky. The sky was gray and dull.

Then Anne was lying next to me and then we were looking at each other, all kind of dreamy like. Or that's what I thought anyway. So I decided to try to kiss her.

"Don't," she said.

"Oh, sorry," I said.

She sat up. "God!" She was scowling at me.

"Sorry."

She stood up and started walking. I got up and started walking after her.

"Wait up," I said.

She stopped and waited for me.

"Sorry," I said.

"Whatever."

We started walking again. I didn't know where we were going.

"Oh great," she said, looking at her shoe.

"What?"

"I think I stepped in dog shit."

She had all this orange stuff on her shoe. You could smell it. Definitely dog shit.

"Gross," she said.

She started wiping her shoe on the grass. I looked around for a stick or something. I found a plastic bag and handed it to her.

"What's that for?"

"Your shoe."

Then she just started laughing at me.

"What?" I said. "You don't want it?" I was just standing there holding the plastic bag like a total idiot.

She shook her head. Finally she said, "Come on, let's go."

We didn't really talk much on the train ride back to Florence. I mostly pretended to sleep. I was embarrassed and annoyed at the same time. So what was that, anyway? Kissing your sister? Your almost step-sister?

I swear though, for a second she had kissed back. Or it seemed that way. I don't know. But she probably hated me now, or at least thought I was a dork.

I sat up and looked out the window. The sun was starting to set and the sky was pinkish blue.

Anne said, "You can still smell it, can't you?"

"What?" I said.

"The dog shit."

"No," I lied.

Twenty-Seven

Sunday I had to confront the fact that I had a paper to write. I hadn't been to class for over a week and hadn't done the reading. I leafed through my books and tried to think of something I could say about stuff that happened five-hundred years earlier.

Then I had an idea. It was a stupid idea, but it was something I could probably milk a few pages out of. So I was actually writing when I heard someone crying. At first I thought I was hearing things, but then I put down my book and listened closely. It was definitely crying, and it seemed to be coming from within the apartment.

I got up and opened my door. It was coming from down the hall.

I walked far enough down the hall to be sure it was coming from Sr. Gasperi's room. There was sobbing, interspersed with muttering.

I remembered hearing my mom cry in her room after she and my dad split up. I remember just standing there outside her door, useless. And suddenly I felt bad for hating Sr. Gasperi so much. She was miserable. Still, what could I do about it?

I wandered back down the hall and into the kitchen, which smelled like moldy sponge and burned coffee.

Dishes were piled in the sink. I felt like a prowler. What was I doing here, anyway? I had to get out of this place.

I walked back into my room and then went out onto the balcony. It was a long way down to the courtyard below, with a bunch of potted plants and scattered chairs. The railing was short and flimsy. I thought about Anne's friend who had jumped off that building. That took a lot. Or maybe it took nothing at all.

Somehow, I finished the paper. My basic argument was that the Renaissance was just a bunch of hype, that sure there were some cool buildings and some funky art, but it did nothing to change anything for 99% percent of the population. It was totally lame, but at least I'd have something to turn in. Maybe I'd get a D but I doubt he could fail me for this. I was still determined to pass, to get by, to get this college thing over with.

Gary got home late that night. He dumped his backpack on the floor and fell onto his bed.

"How was it?" I said.

"Awesome," he said.

"Yeah, did they rock?"

"It was practically religious," he said. "But you don't care."

"I care," I said.

"We're going to see them in Bologna next month."

"Cool," I said.

He rolled onto his side and looked at me. "So what did you do over the weekend?"

I thought about the weird Pisa trip with Anne, about my lame paper, about Sr. Gasperi crying, about my decision to try to get out of this apartment and away from Sr. Gasperi and Gary.

"Nothing," I said.

Twenty-Eight

I got up in time to go to class with Gary. The Renaissance History prof seemed surprised to see me, and even more surprised when I handed him my paper. I went to the back of the class and looked out the window while he lectured on some painter or something.

Wendy and Amy were bitching about the Buddhist at lunch. They really seemed pissed off this time. They'd wanted hot baths after their sixteen-hour train ride back from Amsterdam, but when they got home the Buddhist was hogging the bathroom with her boyfriend and having loud sex in the tub. To top it off there had been nothing for breakfast the next morning.

Amy said, "I already talked to Daniella." (Daniella was the administrator lady.) "They're going to move us."

"Where?" I said.

"I don't care. But they're supposed to move us this week."

"Who's gonna live with the Buddhist?" I said.

They shrugged.

Trish looked at me. "Maybe you should move in there."

"Do it," Gary said.

"Maybe I will," I said.

"You should meet her first," Wendy said.

"Alright," I said. "When?"

"Come over tomorrow night. She's having one of her Buddhism meetings. She's always trying to get us to invite people so she can convert them."

"What do they do at the meeting?"

"They sit around and talk for a while, then they chant."

"Sounds fun," I said.

"Yeah," Amy said, rolling her eyes.

I was dreading seeing Anne after the whole Pisa fiasco, but she didn't seem pissed at me or anything. In fact, nothing seemed different as far as I could tell, but then I'm pretty clueless when in comes to this kind of thing. I told her the latest with the Buddhist and she said, "That sounds awesome. Are you going to chant?"

"Definitely," I said. "Hey, do you want to come?"

"I would, but I'm meeting your roommate to work on our project."

"Oh," I said. Then I said, "Wait, what?"

"He didn't tell you? We have this huge project for art history."

"No," I said. "He didn't tell me."

"Yeah, it really sucks. The project is totally stupid. Plus, I hate working with other people on things."

"Oh," I said.

Gary? Hanging out with Anne? I wasn't sure what to think about this.

"So do you think she'll try to convert you?" Anne said.

"What?" I said. I was still thinking about Gary and Anne.

"Do you think she'll try to convert you to Buddhism?"

"I hope so," I said. "Maybe I'll become a monk."

Twenty-Nine

The meeting with the Buddhists was at eight so I decided to skip dinner with Sr. Gasperi and eat somewhere in Centro. I found a bistro with weird orange curtains and ate another thin pizza and drank a bunch of wine.

I was curious to finally meet this Buddhist woman. Wendy and Amy had never referred to her by her name, so it was surprising to learn that her name was Gina, which didn't really sound like a Buddhist's name. I guess she was also a curator at one of the museums, so she was like an arty Buddhist or something. Anyway, Wendy and Amy weren't going to be there, so I'd be on my own.

I finished the bottle of wine and then went to find the bus. Gina lived on the other side of town from Sr. Gasperi, in a much older, classier-looking neighborhood. I found the address and got buzzed into a foyer with lots of mirrors and marble and healthy-looking plants. I couldn't believe Wendy and Amy had bitched about this.

Gina answered the door. She was thin and pale, with a sharp-looking nose and hair down to her butt, and she was dressed completely in black. Kind of an arty Elvira vibe. When she saw me she smiled and clapped her hands together. "Kevin! Very nice to meet you."

Gina knew English. This was another complaint from Wendy and Amy—that she spoke English to them. I didn't have a problem with it. She spoke it with an English accent, which was kind of hilarious.

She led me into a small living room and introduced me to several people. There were two German guys who spoke good English, and Gina's Argentinean boyfriend Oscar, who also spoke English. And then several nice middle-aged looking Italians who just smiled and nodded at me. They started the meeting right after I arrived.

The meeting only lasted about an hour or so and wasn't terribly formal. I sat in the edge of the couch and drank wine with the Germans and talked to them about living in Florence (Oscar had disappeared a few minutes into the meeting). There was Wolf, who was studying architecture, and Johan, who was an artist of some kind—I wasn't really sure. They were from Hamburg and had only been in Florence for a few months. There was some story about how they had met Gina—something involving a pig or something—I didn't really follow it. Anyway, they weren't into the Buddhism thing but found it curious and amusing.

After a while the others tried to draw me back into the conversation about Buddhism, with Gina translating. They explained that they weren't practicing traditional Buddhism. It seemed to be a strange, almost selfish Buddhism—they chanted so they could get stuff. This older guy explained how chanting had helped him find an apartment. Another woman had solved some money problems. It all seemed kind of strange to me, but I was pretty drunk on wine, so I was cool with it.

And then it was time to chant. There seemed to be no question that I would join them. I followed everyone into Gina's bedroom, where there was a small altar. We sat on the floor and Gina led us into the chant of "nam myoho renge kyo" over and over and over. (I found out later it means "I devote myself to mystical law" or something like that.)

Chanting was actually kind of cool once you got into the rhythm of it. Gina sounded pretty fucking impressive—her voice seemed to come from somewhere deep inside her, and she varied the tempo a bit to keep it interesting. But I admit I got bored after about five minutes and kept checking my watch until it finally ended. Then we all got up and smiled at each other while stretching our stiff legs and backs. Everyone was very eager to hear what I thought. I just smiled a lot and said, "Molto bene," and that seemed to make everyone happy.

After the Italians left, Gina brought up Wendy and Amy and how they were leaving. Then she said, "But you will move in with me, no?" Like it was already decided.

"Sure," I said.

"Good, good."

Of course American students were major cash cows. This was purely a business thing. But I was hoping it would be better than the Sr. Gasperi situation.

Then she showed me Wendy and Amy's room, which was a palace compared to the squalid room I shared with

Gary. It had super tall ceilings and these cool old windows looking out onto the street. It was decorated by Oscar's paintings—abstract smears of color on torn bits of cardboard. I complimented the paintings and Gina looked very pleased.

Later, the Germans drove me home in their little Renault, which seemed like it was going to shake apart every time Wolf hit the brakes. They asked me a bunch of questions about California, and Wolf told me about his trip hitchhiking through the South and Southwest. I liked those dudes. They seemed like good guys. And when they dropped me off, my neighborhood seemed even more dull, if that was possible.

Thirty

And so it was all arranged. I moved in with Gina that Saturday. It was almost too easy. I just packed my backpack, took the bus over and let myself in with the key Wendy had given me the day before. Gina wasn't even around—she was down in Naples visiting her sister. So I had the place to myself.

The fridge was pretty well stocked. Gina even drank normal non-carbonated water. Still, it was all Italian-type stuff and I wanted something else. Luckily, there was a little grocery store a block away. It was like a real supermarket, in miniature. They even had little grocery carts. I was stoked. I had been dreaming about Top Ramen and burritos, but I ended up buying some chicken and potatoes and a six pack of Heineken—the Budweiser of Europe. Then I went back to the apartment and made myself a feast.

After stuffing myself I went and turned on the TV and flipped through the channels until I found *The Streets of San Francisco*. I watched the young Michael Douglas dubbed into Italian and let out a bunch of Heineken burps. I was starting to feel like an actual human again.

Thirty-One

Wendy and Amy were super excited about their new place. I guess the host family woman was a really good cook, plus they got to have a giant bathroom all to themselves. They didn't seem overly curious about how I was doing with Gina. Wendy asked me if I could retrieve a bottle of shampoo she'd left behind.

Meanwhile, something was up with Gary and Trish. During lunch there were a bunch of odd silences, and then Trish got up from the table and walked off with her food half-eaten. Amy followed after her but then came back a few minutes later and shrugged. Gary was just sitting there, reading one of his art history books.

I got a letter from my buddy Joey in Las Vegas. He was making lots of cash as a baccarat dealer and dating a six-foot-tall showgirl with breast implants. I felt completely jealous and depressed. He enclosed a few hits of acid with little clown faces. Joey and I had done quite a bit of acid in high school, but he said this stuff was "a new level of depravity"—whatever that meant.

There was also a message from my dad. He was going to be in Florence in three weeks. It was hard to believe.

I was supposed to call him back.

Oh, and I got my paper back in Renaissance History. The prof had made a few comments to let me know that he knew it was a total copout, but he was letting me get away with it. He gave me a C+. I was stoked.

I saw Anne in political science. I still didn't know what was up with us after the Pisa incident. Then there was the whole thing with Gary and the art project. Gary had found out that my dad was dating Anne's mom and had asked me a whole bunch of questions. It had been kind of annoying, especially when he said, "so she's practically your stepsister." I couldn't tell if he was interested in her or what.

Anne seemed to be acting like nothing had happened. She said, "So how's the Buddhist?"

"Fine, I guess. I haven't really seen her. She's gone for the weekend." Then I said, "So how did the art project go?"

"Fine," Anne said.

"That's good."

"Why?" Anne said.

"I don't know."

"Gary actually did a pretty good job."

"Cool," I said. And I felt like a jealous dork.

Anne and I walked out together. As it turned out, my new bus stop was in the same direction as her place.

"My mom is being so irritating right now."

"Why?" I said. "What's up?"

She rolled her eyes. "Every time we talk she starts complaining about your dad."

"Tell her to dump his ass."

Anne laughed.

"Seriously, she should," I said. "Then maybe we'd be saved from a visit."

"No, I think she's holding on just for the vacation," Anne said.

"Great."

We walked past this Chinese restaurant. It was pretty close to the Duomo but for some reason I hadn't seen it before.

I said, "Do you think they're actually Chinese, or is it Italians cooking Chinese food?"

"I don't know," Anne said. "But we should try it."

"No way."

"What? It would be funny."

"I think I can wait another month or so to have Chinese food."

"Scared?" Anne said.

"No. It just seems wrong or something."

"Oh come on. Why is it any weirder than a Chinese restaurant in the US?"

"I don't know. It just is."

"Why?"

"I don't know," I said.

"Come on, I dare you to eat there with me."

"Fine," I said.

She wanted to shake on it. What was the deal with this hand shake pact stuff, anyway? I didn't get it.

We walked a bit farther til we came to a street where she had to turn off. She said, "I'm this way." The way she said it, it almost was like she wanted me to follow her. And then she was just looking at me with this goofy look on her face. Did she want me to kiss her again? Was it some kind of trap? Or a test? But there was no way I was going to make the first move again.

Then, abruptly, she said, "Bye." And walked off.

I walked back to my bus stop. I would never understand chicks. Or anyway I would never understand the chicks that I always seemed to be interested in. Why was that?

When I got back to the apartment Oscar was there with the Germans. They were playing Bruce Springsteen and moving paintings around the apartment.

"You guys like Bruce Springsteen?" I said.

Wolf shouted, "The Boss!" and Johan jumped up on the couch and played air guitar. Then "Born in the USA" came on and they all started singing along.

"Okay, okay," I said.

Oscar had a new series of paintings of baby dolls with empty eye sockets. I ended up with two of the baby doll paintings in my room—with their empty eyes staring at me. It was kind of creepy, but kind of cool, too. I'm sure Wendy and Amy would have freaked.

A while later Gina came home and we all had dinner. Oscar was an amazing chef. He made some kind of crazy beef stew thing and we drank a bunch of wine. The Germans didn't leave til after midnight.

I was lying in bed drunk and half asleep when I heard the sex noises. At first I had no idea what it was—somehow I'd forgotten about Wendy and Amy's stories. It started with a low moaning sound, but then Gina started shrieking. It sounded like Oscar was murdering her. And it went on and on and on. Holy shit. I could see how this could get old. I put my head under the pillow and tried to sleep.

Thirty-Two

Gina and I were hanging out before dinner when she asked me if I wanted to chant. For some reason it hadn't occurred to me that chanting was going to be part of the deal. Maybe I had actually seemed interested at the meeting. Or maybe she really wanted to convert me. Anyway, I couldn't think of an excuse, so I agreed.

We went to Gina's room and sat on the chanting mat in front of her little shrine.

As we chanted I kept sneaking peeks at her. She was wearing this tight black leotard and her breasts were clearly defined through the sheer material. I have to admit she was pretty damn hot looking.

On the whole, living there was pretty good. I couldn't complain. There were still a few issues, though.

First off, I was bummed to discover that Gina also had one of those squat-style shower setups, but I guess it was pretty much standard issue in Italy—and anyway I'd gotten fairly used to it by then.

One other thing about Gina: her hair was everywhere—the sink, the shower, the toilet, even in my food. Maybe she was shedding or something. I couldn't figure it out. But it was kind of gross.

Also, Gina and Oscar seemed to argue a lot. They'd yell at each other a bit, and then they wouldn't talk to each other for a while. Later they'd go have loud makeup sex.

Meanwhile, the Germans were in the middle of planning a big party they were having on Friday. Wolf wanted me to invite every American girl from the program. I tried to explain that most of them were super annoying, but he didn't seem to care.

Wolf had a DJ all signed up for the party and was trying to figure out how to get all the DJ's crap over to the party. Apparently there were some large amps and some other stuff that wouldn't fit in the little Renault.

Without really thinking about it I volunteered Antonio and his Ape. I hadn't seen Antonio in a while but figured he'd be up for it. It was a party after all, and Antonio was a party type of guy. Of course the best way to get Antonio to agree to it would be to invite Wendy and Amy, which might be tricky since Gina would be there. I was pretty sure I'd figure it out, though.

Thirty-Three

I met Antonio at "La Bellissima" a few hours before the party. The Germans were supposed to come by when they were ready and then we'd follow them in the Ape to go to pick up the DJ's shit.

As I'd predicted, Antonio was totally excited to go to the party once he found out I'd invited Wendy. And also as I'd predicted, Wendy and Amy hadn't been all that thrilled about coming after they heard that Gina would be there, but I'd managed to convince them anyway.

Antonio and I drank grappa while we waited for the Germans to show up. Then his buddies Roberto and Mateo showed up and we drank more. I liked those guys, but they didn't know any English so Antonio was always having to translate their lame jokes. I don't know, maybe the jokes were funnier in Italian.

By the time the Germans finally arrived Antonio and I were drunk. Wolf, Johan and Antonio all shook hands, and then Wolf told us to follow them. Antonio and I went out and got into the Ape.

"You drive," Antonio said. "I drunk."

"Alright," I said.

I sat behind the wheel. Only, it wasn't a wheel. It was like the handlebars on my mod buddy's Vespa. I had no idea how to drive the thing.

There was a thud and the Ape rocked violently as Roberto and Mateo climbed in back. I guess they were coming to the party, too.

Antonio reached across me and started up the two stroke engine. Wolf's Renault was already disappearing into traffic. I twisted the throttle and the Ape started bucking madly—I guess I wasn't quite used to the clutch. One of Antonio's buddies bashed into the back of the cab and swore. Then the clutch seemed to engage and we lurched violently forward into the street.

There was a yell behind us and then Antonio shouted, "Stop!"

I squeezed the brakes and turned around.

Roberto was laughing his ass off and yelling insults at Mateo, who was sitting up in the middle of the road with his legs splayed out like Charlie Chaplan. He was giving us all the emphatic Italian finger.

"Oops," I said.

"I drive," Antonio said.

The DJ's place was all the way across town. The DJ was this real slick-looking Moroccan dude wearing white shoes and sunglasses. He didn't seem very impressed with the Ape. We spent half an hour convincing him it would work, and another half hour tying down the amps, speakers and strobe light shit—we had to re-do it like five times before he was satisfied.

It had been freezing outside recently. Luckily, Gina had lent me a long wool trench coat. It buttoned up the wrong way and smelled like her but it was warm.

Finally the DJ's gear was all set and we drove over to the German's place. The DJ rode with Antonio in the Ape and I grabbed a ride in the Renault, sandwiched between Roberto and Mateo. Mateo was complaining that his ass still hurt from falling out of the back of the Ape. Roberto made fun of him and complimented me on my excellent driving skills.

"You Niki Lauda," Roberto said.

"Who?"

"Niki Lauda," he said. "Molto famoso. Ferrari. Formula Uno."

"Oh," I said. "Right."

The Germans lived in a big industrial-looking flat over a bakery. It was about a block from some train tracks grown over with weeds. There was a soccer field behind it with a half-collapsed goalpost.

Anne and Susan were waiting out front. Our convoy had arrived about an hour later than I had told them we'd be there. Oops. Anne was wearing a huge white parka with a fur lining. She looked like an Eskimo.

"Hey!" Anne said.

"What's up?" I said.

"Nothing," Anne said. "Just standing out here in the cold."

"Sorry," I said.

"Nice coat," Anne said.

"Likewise," I said.

The DJ and the Germans were already busy unloading crap and pulling it inside. I would have helped but I felt like shit. I was at that point where you have to make the decision to either keep drinking or go to bed. I was seriously thinking of trying to find a place to go to sleep.

Antonio came up and made me introduce him to Anne and Susan. I could tell he wasn't overly impressed by either of them. Then he asked when Wendy was getting there. I told him I didn't know. He patted me on the back and wandered inside.

It took another hour for the DJ to set up. Anne and Susan and I were just standing around, drinking sour-tasting wine out of paper cups. The Germans finally got the strobe lights going, then the DJ put on some lame-sounding Euro techno music.

"Wow," Anne said.

"Yeah," I said.

"Someone should really tell them that this music sucks," Anne said.

"Ignorance is bliss," I said.

"No, ignorance is just ignorance," Anne said.

A while later Gary and Wendy and Amy showed up. They walked up to us and we all nodded at each other and said, "Hey." Still no sign or mention of Trish. Gary and Anne started talking about something to do with their art history class.

Soon Antonio came bouncing up and dragged Wendy off to dance. Gary and Anne were still talking about their stupid class. Amy and Susan just looked glum.

Eventually Oscar and Gina arrived, followed by a bunch of other random people I'd never seen before. It was almost midnight and the party was finally starting to happen.

There seemed to be lots of Germans. There were also some Italian transvestites. I guess there was a big transvestite scene in Florence. Who knew? It's not something that gets mentioned in the guidebooks.

I talked to this one guy who was wearing a velour jumpsuit. We got into this discussion about dentists and dentistry. He had some theory about Americans and teeth that I didn't really follow.

I was feeling pretty crappy. Wine did that to me. I switched to the vodka punch Johan had made, which made it worse. Why couldn't these people drink beer? I mean, shit, they were Germans.

I went back to talk to Anne and Gary and Amy and Susan. Gary and Anne had stopped talking about their stupid art history class. Now Gary was talking about the next U2 show, which was in Bologna. I guess it was the same weekend as our class trip to Rome.

It was kind of weird to see them all getting along like this after the crazy clique-like behavior during lunch. I guess alcohol helps. Still, I couldn't really figure Anne out. Did she like these people now?

Then Anne said, "I hope they play some stuff from October. That's my favorite U2 album."

"That's their worst album," Gary said.

"No it's not!" Anne said.

"Wait," I said. "You're going to U2?"

"Maybe," she said. "Why?"

"I don't know," I said.

Gary said, "You okay, man?"

"Yeah," I said. "Why?"

He laughed. "You look kind of pissed off."

They were all looking at me. I just shrugged.

I decided to go outside. A train was going past slowly. Clackity clackity clack. I walked out onto the soccer field and sat near the midfield line.

It was dark and quiet and cold. I was kind of happy, just sitting out in that field wearing Gina's warm coat and looking up at the sky. There were even a few stars out. I tried not to think about Anne.

For some reason I started thinking about that cat we had fed in Siena. I wondered how it was doing. It was probably strong and healthy now—it had probably gone on to father another litter of starving kittens. Or maybe it was dead.

I wondered what Sr. Gasperi was doing tonight. Probably snoring in bed. And what was my dad doing? I guess it was the middle of the afternoon for him. Shit, I was supposed to call him back. I just didn't feel like it.

As the noise of the train faded I noticed this digging sound. I couldn't see anything at first, but then finally I spotted a rodent of some kind—probably a gopher—just a few yards away. He was really going to town over there. Moving mountains of dirt.

"Hi Mr. Gopher," I said. I felt like Bill Murray. But a peaceful Bill Murray.

The gopher froze for a second and looked at me. It didn't seem terribly impressed. It went back to its digging.

I watched from my place in the middle of the field as Anne and Susan left with Gary and Amy in a cab. A few minutes later I saw Antonio and Wendy leave in the Ape.

The gopher had disappeared. I was starting to get a second wind so I went back to see who was still inside.

Roberto and Mateo were still there, along with some Germans and transvestites. They were playing Blondie. I went and got another glass of punch.

* * *

I woke up the next morning on the floor with Johan standing over me.

"We go get coffee," he said.

"Okay," I said.

"We wait for you."

It took me a good minute or so to get up. One whole side of my body was completely stiff from sleeping on the floor. And my shoes were missing. Finally, I found them on top of one of the speakers.

I stumbled out into the blinding sunshine and followed them to the cafe. I was incredibly thirsty and felt like I was going to puke.

The café was about a block away. I got an espresso and a glass of water. I steadied myself on the bar. I drank the water but then couldn't face the espresso. I wanted to go back to bed.

Wolf pointed to my feet and laughed and said, "You were crazy last night."

"I was?"

They told me how I had taken off my shoes and started doing long slides across the floor in my stocking feet. I guess that explained the missing shoes.

Then they told me that the DJ was pissed that Antonio had disappeared with the Ape. He was going to charge them extra now.

"You shouldn't pay him," I said. "He sucked."

Johan shook his head. "No. The music was very good."

Wolf nodded. "Very good."

I shrugged. I didn't feel like arguing with a bunch of Germans.

Thirty-Four

A week went by. After the Germans' party I was feeling sick of everyone.

I was doing a lot of skating. Gina's neighborhood had some cool shit. Italians would stop and watch me like I was Christian Hosoi or something. It was cool.

I got some new batteries for my walkman. I also found this music store that sold Western music. Of course I couldn't find anything really cool, so I ended up buying a bunch of random crap I'd been into when I was in middle school. I got AC/DC Dirty Deeds Done Dirt Cheap and Scorpions Blackout. And, for no good reason, I also go Guns N' Roses Appetite for Destruction (no way you would have been able to talk me into that in the States, but it seemed funny here). I paid like twice what I would have paid in the US, but what could I do—I was desperate.

Back at the apartment, it was the same old shit. The Germans were always there, Gina's long black hair was everywhere, and she and Oscar would fight and then have loud sex. Still, it was better than dealing with Sr. Gasperi and Gary, so I tried not to stress about it too much.

School was just kind of annoying. What I'd first noticed at the Germans' party seemed to hold true for the whole group now—people were starting to blend together more and act less clique-ish. Probably cause we were only three or four weeks away from never seeing each other again. It had gotten like that in the last few months of my senior year of high school—suddenly the jocks were hanging out with the hippies and the punk rockers were hanging out with the metal heads. Big kumbaya fest.

The vibe within our own little lunch clique had deteriorated quite a bit. Gary and Trish were definitely over, so that had thrown things out of whack. Trish was acting kind of weird—too happy or something. And Gary seemed to have a new attitude. He'd been acting kind of affected—he'd started growing a goatee and had bought an acoustic guitar which he'd carry around with him. I wasn't sure what Amy and Wendy thought of all of this. I wasn't even sure if the two of them were getting along anymore, either. Maybe that had something to do with Antonio.

And then there was Anne. I had no idea what was going on there. Half of me had given up on anything happening between us. The other half still held out some hope.

The big Rome trip was just around the corner. I was actually kind of excited about it. I really wanted to see the Roman ruins and Colosseum and Vatican and stuff. I was saving the LSD Joey had sent me for the Sistine Chapel. Seemed like the perfect place to trip out.

Thirty-Five

We came in by the Colosseum. I have to admit I was pretty blown away. The Leaning Tower had been a goofy anticlimax, but the Colosseum was fucking incredible. It's hard to explain if you haven't seen it, but it was damn cool—especially after all the wussy Renaissance shit.

They put us in this huge old hotel on Corso Vittorio Emmanuel II. We'd talked about Emmanuel II in political science—the first king of Italy, who unified Italy in like 1860 or something. So he got a street named after him in pretty much every town in Italy.

Anyway, the hotel was cool. It had crazy high ceilings and this orange carpet that probably hadn't been cleaned since 1970 or something. People tossed their backpacks and duffels all over the floor and flopped on chairs and couches while the administrator lady figured stuff out.

By default, I ended up with Gary as my roommate again. It seemed kind of weird at this point, but it would only be for two days—we were heading to Assisi on Sunday. And anyway it wasn't like we were going to be hanging out in the room a whole lot together.

After we'd dumped our crap in our rooms and listened to a spiel about curfew, they turned us loose for dinner.

It's nearly impossible to cross the street in Rome. There are angry hordes of Fiats everywhere. So we were all huddled together on the sidewalk, afraid to step into the street. Our group had really stood out in Florence or Siena. But here we just seemed small and lame, pushed to the side. Rome would either ignore us or swallow us whole.

We seriously stood there for like two or three minutes, trying to figure out how to cross. Finally I saw this young Italian girl casually wade out in traffic. She got across no problem. I decided to do the same. I just stepped off the curb and started walking. All the cars came to a screeching halt. So then everyone followed. I felt like Moses or something.

After we crossed the street people faded in different directions. I ended up at the Pantheon with Gary and the chicks. The Pantheon is a huge Roman building with a hole in the ceiling. I didn't really get the whole hole concept, but whatever. I guess it could be cool to go there sometime when it was raining. But of course it was closed so we couldn't go inside. Not that anyone really wanted to—we were all hungry and talking about where to eat.

Then I saw the McDonald's. I couldn't believe there was a McDonald's right across from the Pantheon.

"Let's go to McDonald's," I said.

"No way," Gary said.

"Why not?" I said.

"It's too American," Gary said.

"What does that mean?" I said. "Anyway, it looks like there are a bunch of Italians in there."

"That's not the point," Gary said.

"Think about how good a Big Mac would taste right now," I said. "What, no one wants to go?"

They all just stared at me.

"Fine," I said.

I went and waited in line with a bunch of Italians. It was funny, I couldn't remember the last time I'd eaten at McDonald's. There had been a Jack in the Box next to my place in Davis, and I'd gone there all the time when I was stoned. I liked their crappy tacos. I'd eat like five of them at a time.

I decided to just go with the Big Mac. It seemed to be what everyone else was ordering. And when in Rome... I took my Big Mac and fries and Coke and sat down.

McDonald's tastes different in Italy. Maybe it was me, or maybe I had gotten too used to Italian food, but the Big Mac tasted weird. Kind of sweet or something, and the bread didn't seem quite right. It was still good, though. And the tall icy Coke was awesome.

I caught back up with everyone at this trattoria nearby. They were sitting outside even though it was cold, eating pizza and drinking wine.

"How was your Big Mac?" Trish said.

"Excellent."

The whole piazza was lit up and lots of people were walking around and talking. There were fewer tourists in Rome—more Italians and not so many damned mopeds. So it was pretty cool.

After a while the conversation turned to the Vatican.

Gary was really excited about it—he was saying it would be the high point of his whole trip, if not his life.

"But aren't you a Protestant?" I said.

"Episcopalian," Gary said.

"I thought Protestants hated Catholics. I thought that was the whole point of being a Protestant."

"That's not true at all," Gary said.

"Oh," I said.

After we finished dinner we walked over to the Piazza Navona, which has this huge fountain with a bunch of mermen blowing water through seashells.

We sat at another outside café and ordered wine. Or everyone else ordered wine and I managed to get a beer. Then these Italian guys walked over to us and started flirting with the chicks. It was annoying but funny, too. Gary's Italian was better than anyone else's and he was just kind of fucking with them. Then Trish started flirting with this one guy who was wearing a sailor outfit. Gary pretended like he didn't care. And maybe he didn't.

Then Anne and Susan and Arnie walked up to us.

"Hey!" Gary said.

"Hi guys," Anne said. "What are you doing?"

"Nothing," Gary said. "What are you doing?"

"Nothing," Anne said.

I guess everyone was still all buddy-buddy. I just couldn't get used to it.

Then the guy with the sailor outfit invited us all to some bar and everyone agreed to go. I was surprised that Arnie and Susan didn't beg off at that point.

The bar was even lamer than Antonio's chrome bar, but a lot more rowdy and with more Italian guys—a bunch of them in sailor suits. Actually, the guy to chick ratio was kind of scary—I was kind of worried for the American girls with us.

Then Anne said, "Want to go outside? It's so hot in here."

"Okay," I said.

When we got outside, Anne took out a pack of cigarettes and started whacking them in that annoying smoker's manner. Finally, she lit her cigarette, but then she didn't smoke it. She started chewing her nails instead.

She was looking really good right then, and I wanted to kiss her again but didn't want a repeat of Pisa. I didn't want to be a pleading, whiny loser. This whole thing sucked.

Finally she said, "Rome is so amazing."

"Yeah," I said.

She looked at me but she wasn't thinking about me. She was thinking about something else. I had no idea what, though.

"So are you having fun?"

"I don't know," I said. "I guess. But it kind of seems like one of those things you'll look back on later and you'll be like, wow, that was kind of cool. But at the time everything mostly seems lame and annoying."

"I'm trying not to be like that."

"That's good," I said. "So you're like all rah-rah now and stuff, huh?"

"Not really. I'm just not a total nihilist like you."

"Thanks."

"We're only here a few more weeks. You should make the most of it."

"Thanks for the tip."

She took a drag on her cigarette and then exhaled. "So I talked to my mom yesterday."

"Yeah? What'd she have to say?"

"Nothing much. They're just getting all ready for their trip."

"That's good."

"I guess your dad's back is acting up?"

"What else is new?"

"I'm actually looking forward to it."

"That's good," I said.

Then I heard U2 come on in the bar. I remembered that conversation at the Germans' party.

"You're seriously going to U2?"

"I don't know. Why?"

"I don't know."

"Arnie's going, too," she said.

"You're kidding."

"You should come along. It's going to be fun."

I shrugged.

"Oh come on, don't be such a party pooper. Why don't you want to go?"

"To see U2?"

"Oh come on. U2 isn't that bad."

"Yeah they are," I said.

She shrugged. "Alright. Suit yourself." She stamped out her cigarette. "Let's go back inside," she said.

Things got even crazier at the bar. More Italian guys and more Americans. At one point Dana brushed up against me. She was with some short balding guy I didn't recognize. He wasn't from our program but seemed to be American. He was wearing a Harvard sweatshirt and an expensive-looking watch.

"Hi," she said.

"Hi," I said.

"How's it going?" she said.

"Good," I said.

"Good," she said. Then she laughed and walked away.

Hey, whatever. Fine with me.

I ended up walking back to the hotel with Susan. Anne and Arnie and Gary and the chicks had wanted to stay even though it was past curfew.

We were walking down this narrow street with a bunch of shops that had their garage door things pulled down and locked.

"Are we going the right way?" Susan said.

"I think so," I said.

"I don't know."

Then all of a sudden we popped out into the big piazza near the Pantheon.

"Here we go," I said.

We kept walking.

"So Anne just told me you're like stepsiblings or something."

"Not quite."

"That's kind of weird, though."

"Yeah," I said. "I guess."

"I thought you had a crush on her or something." Then she said, "I'm sorry," and started giggling. I think it was the first time I'd see her smile and laugh.

I didn't say anything.

Later I got woken up by chicks screaming in the hallway. I opened the door to see Wendy and Amy trying to calm Trish, who was screaming and laughing.

Then Trish puked. It's funny seeing girls puke. They always act all surprised and embarrassed.

Trish puked again, this time with a lot more quantity.

"Gross," Amy said.

Trish started sobbing.

I closed the door.

Thirty-Six

Everyone was hungover for the trip to the Forum. Trish didn't even make it. Wendy and Amy wore sunglasses to hide their eyes.

The ruins were really cool, but it was kind of hard to picture what ancient Rome had been like. All that was left was pieces of buildings and columns and a few beat-up statues. There was a lot of grass and weeds and dirt and garbage. And cats. Tons of cats. I was kind of worried that Anne would start freaking out about the cats but she didn't say anything.

We were walking past a row of tall columns when something caught my eye.

"Dude, someone carved Metallica in a Roman ruin," I said.

"That's really sad," Anne said.

"What? I said. "I bet Caesar would have liked *Master of Puppets*."

We walked down into a wide-open area. Here you could get a sense of the vastness of it. It was ruins in every direction.

I felt like I was in that movie *Logan's Run* or something. Okay, maybe not *Logan's Run* but something kind of post-apocalyptic like that.

It was weird how my mind always wandered when I was in these hugely famous historical places. I could never seem to be totally "in the moment." Instead I'd think about *Logan's Run* or something retarded like that.

We were staring at remains of something called the "House of the Vestal Virgins" (Arnie was reading from his guidebook) when these gypsy kids came running up to us. They were talking a mile a minute and trying to show us some newspaper—really shoving them in our faces. Before I knew it one of them had his hand in my pocket and was trying to pull out my wallet. I grabbed his arm so that his hand was wedged in my pocket. He started tugging really hard and finally got away from me. He ripped my pants a bit but didn't get my wallet. They ran off.

"You okay?" Anne said.

"Yeah," I said.

Then all of a sudden these two American jock guys ran up to us. One of them was wearing a Redskins cap. The other one had a crewcut and a sunburn.

The one with a Redskins cap said, "Did they get your wallet?"

"No," I said. I was shaking a bit but I thought it was kind of funny, too. It had all happened so fast.

"They got mine," crewcut guy said. "It had my passport."

"That sucks," I said.

"Dammit!" The crewcut guy started stomping around the place and shaking his fists, all angry and stuff. It was kind of comical, and I couldn't help it, I started laughing.

"What are you laughing at?" the crewcut guy said.

"Nothing," I said. But I kept laughing. I couldn't help it.

"Hey, fuck you," the guy said.

"Just calm down, man," the Redskins guy said.

"I'm calm," crewcut guy said. "It's these people."

"Come on." The guy with the Redskins cap started pulling his friend away.

"You people are crazy," crewcut guy said.

"Yeah, we are," I said. "We're fucking crazy!"

"Fuck you," the guy said, but his buddy was dragging him away.

"Crazy!" I said.

Arnie was looking pretty uncomfortable, but Anne started laughing, too.

Next we went to the Colosseum. This was probably the coolest thing I'd seen in Italy. Maybe anywhere.

First we climbed up in the stands. It was kind of like a big stone football stadium. When you looked down there was no field—the arena grounds were gone. Instead it was like you had x-ray vision and could see through the floor and into the cells and cages where they had kept all the tigers and gladiators and whatnot. It was a trip.

Then we walked down into the chambers below the old arena. It was like a big maze, with narrow passages and cages. And of course more garbage and graffiti.

"It's really gross to think about it," Anne said.

"What?"

"Think about all the people and animals that died here."

"It was like two thousand years ago."

Anne didn't say anything, but she looked kind of upset.

I thought about that gypsy kid's bony arm. I wondered if he was already terrorizing some other tourists. Then I thought about the asshole jock guys. Then I tried to think about all the people and animals who had died here, but all I could picture was cheesy Hollywood movies.

So then we were done with the Colosseum. We had almost two hours before we were supposed to all meet up at the Vatican.

We crossed the streets and headed up some vaguely modern looking steps. We went up two long flights but then came to a dead end in front of a wall.

"That's odd," Anne said.

Arnie consulted his guidebook.

"Mussolini built these," he said. "They don't lead anywhere. They're just for show."

"Kind of fitting," Susan said.

Then we noticed that the ground was literally covered with syringes. Looked like a big junky hangout.

"Creepy," Anne said. "Let's get out of here."

Thirty-Seven

Going to the Vatican was like going to a major league baseball game. As you got closer the crowds and noise increased, along with the knickknacks and flags and general Vatican-oriented bullshit. I admit I was excited. It was hard not to be. Even Susan looked excited.

I saw a bottle opener with the Pope on it and had to stop and buy it. It was my first souvenir from Italy. A Popener.

And then everything opened up and we were there. St. Peters. I don't know what I was expecting. It was just a big ass church in the middle of a big ass piazza. Kind of cool I guess, but I'd already seen a lot of churches. This was definitely the biggest, though, no question.

We met the rest of our group in front of the huge obelisk in the middle of the piazza. Obelisk. That was a new word for me. Basically it's a big column. I guess the Romans had dragged it over from Egypt two thousand years ago and stuck it in the middle of some racecourse where they circled around it in chariots and stuff. Then about five hundred years ago a Pope decided he liked it so he dragged it over and put it in front of St. Peters and stuck a cross on top. Looked kind of weird there I thought.

Gary walked over and made a big point of showing Anne these sketches he had made in the ruins. He showed her about ten sketches and she acted all interested. I thought they looked retarded, like something a third grader would draw. I showed Gary the Popener. He didn't seem impressed.

I was all set to take the acid Joey had sent me. I hadn't done acid in a while. It had been a year at least. I was kind of curious what it would do to me. I guess I'd find out soon enough.

Annoying history man had appeared and started running through our itinerary. We were going to go into St. Peters and would spend a while looking at all the stuff. Then we'd go visit the Sistine Chapel and check out the crazy shit on the ceiling. I took the mention of the Sistine Chapel as my cue. I took out the little clown face and put it on my tongue.

LSD is fairly predictable. I'd have five minutes or so before the speed kicked, then another twenty or thirty minutes before the weirdness started. The freak show would last four to six hours, and then I'd begin a slow descent back to normalcy.

St. Peters seems big on the outside but it seems even bigger on the inside. Like really really big. It's hard to explain how huge this thing is. But it made the Florence Duomo seem like a joke.

The speed came on pretty strong and pretty fast. I had to really focus on keeping it together cause I started feeling all hyper and jumpy and wanted to run away. I tried to stay calm and prepare myself for the weirdness to come.

It wasn't long before I felt that subtle shift, and the patterns started to creep up on me. The edges started to bend in and then melt away and the center started to swirl and pulse and kaleidoscope. Joey hadn't been kidding about this stuff.

I realized pretty quickly that St. Peters was the wrong place to take acid. It was sensory overload. Too many patterns, too much weird shit. I mean, there were a bunch of tombs and scary looking statues all over the place. And the echoey noises were freaky. I was getting overwhelmed. I decided I better find a place to sit down.

I went over to this quiet side area and slid into some pews. The pews were cool. They were cool and dark. Worn down by a million asses over a million years. I guess I was inspired by all the religious crap cause I said a prayer. I prayed I wouldn't lose my mind. And I prayed that if I did lose my mind I would find it again.

Someone had left a candy wrapper on the seat. It was an Italian candy wrapper—gold and red and silver around the edges. It crinkled better than a Jolly Rancher wrapper, better than a Tootsie Roll wrapper. I held it up to my ear and crinkled it, and then crinkled it some more. It was cool.

"Kevin?"

Wendy and Amy were standing over me.

"Yeah?" I said.

"What are you doing?"

"Nothing." I hid the candy wrapper behind my back.

"You were talking to yourself."

"No I wasn't."

"Are you okay?"

"Yeah," I said.

Amy's face was scaring me. Something about her eyeliner. Or maybe her eyes. They were kind of bulging. I couldn't look at them.

"We're going to the Sistine Chapel now."

"Oh," I said. "Right."

I didn't want to get up. I didn't want to go anywhere.

"Come on," Amy said. "Let's go." Like my mommy.

"Okay," I said.

I followed them. I didn't look around at the tombs or sculptures or whatever other crap was pulsing and flashing and generally laughing at me. And I definitely didn't look at the floor. The floor was the worst. It was moving. A bunch of geometric shapes flowing over and into each other.

I focused on Amy's pink purse. It was made out of bubble gum. Or taffy. I looked at my hands. I was Gumby. No I wasn't. Gumby is green. Pokey is orange. So I was Pokey. But Pokey is a horse.

We were in line for the Sistine Chapel. It was like waiting in line for a rock concert or roller coaster or a George Lucas movie.

"What's so funny?" Anne said.

"What?"

"You keep laughing."

"Oh yeah," I said.

The line started moving.

"Here we go," Wendy said.

And we were in.

I'm not really sure what happened in there. I remember seeing the thing with God and Adam reaching out to touch fingers. I got kind of tripped out by all the cracks in the ceiling. But then I got to The Last Judgment. It was all fine and good until I found that picture of one guy holding the skin of another dude who looks like he has been flayed. I guess the flayed dude was supposed to be Michelangelo's self-portrait, but it also looked kind of like my dad, and I freaked. Later Wendy told me I started moaning. Amy said I was crying. Then I left.

After that I kind of lost track of things. I lost track of everyone from the group. Then I got completely lost in the Vatican museums. I didn't know where I was. I ended up in a staircase that was like the inside of a seashell. I was going down. Might have been the seashell to hell. I was in the bowels of the Vatican. That was funny. Bowels of the Vatican. Tidy bowl. The Pope was the Tidy Bowl man. He was Mr. Clean. Where was he anyway? I thought he'd be around. I was kind of hoping for an autograph.

I was sitting in a corner by some bathrooms when an Italian rent-a-cop told me to leave. Or I think that's what he said. The walkie-talkie on his shoulder was squawking like a parrot. And I'm pretty sure his gun was plastic.

Later I was outside, sitting on a curb. It was nice outside. I was using a broken Bic pen to dig stuff out from between the cobblestones. Did you know Bic is an

Italian company? I bet not. Anyway, I was finding a lot of bottle caps. I found lots and lots of bottle caps in all different colors.

It got late. I decided I better go back to the hotel. I don't know how I found my way back, but somehow I got back onto good old Emmanuel II and followed him back to the hotel.

Red beard man was there when I walked in. He said, "What's in your pockets?"

"What?" I said. Then I looked down at my pockets. They were bulging with bottle caps. I was like a fucking squirrel with these things. Only, a squirrel would have them in his cheeks, and I had them in my pockets. And my hands were filthy. Jesus my hands were filthy.

I remembered I had been asked a question.

"Bottle caps," I said. I removed two large handfuls from my pockets. Some of them fell onto the floor. "You want some?"

"Why would I want a bunch of dirty bottle caps?"

"I don't know," I said.

"Are you high?"

"What makes you say that?" Then I started laughing. I couldn't stop.

I went up to my room. The patterns were finally starting to chill out. I arranged my bottle caps neatly on my bed. I sorted by color, then re-sorted by age and condition.

I was thirsty. I kind of wanted a beer or something. But I was scared to leave the room. I thought of calling room service but I couldn't find a phone.

Gary came back to the room. "Where did you go?"

"I don't know."

"Everyone is talking about you."

"Oh yeah?" I said. "What are they saying?"

"They said they thought you were on drugs."

"I am on drugs." Then I said, "What do you think of my bottle cap collection?"

He didn't look very impressed.

"Are you thirsty?" I said.

"No," he said.

"Oh," I said.

"I think doing drugs in the Vatican is disgusting. It's disrespectful."

"Okay," I said.

"That's all you can say?"

I shrugged.

"Whatever," Gary said. And then he left.

A while later someone knocked on the door.

"Yeah?" I said.

Anne opened the door part-way. "Hey," she said. "You're alive."

"Yep."

I felt like shit. I didn't feel like talking to anyone. Why couldn't people leave me alone?

Then I saw Susan and Arnie standing behind her, just kind of peering in at me. Arnie made some kind of comment and Susan laughed.

"What did you say?" I said.

"Nothing," Arnie said.

"No," I said. "What did you say?"

"Nothing."

"Fuck you," I said. "Fuck all of you." I got up and closed the door on them. Fuck them. Fuck everyone.

I went and sat back on my bed, which messed up my neat rows of bottle caps. I pushed the rest of them onto the floor and got under the covers. With my shoes on.

Thirty-Eight

In the morning they told us to pack our stuff and put it downstairs so it could be loaded onto the bus. We were going to spend the morning over at some place called the Spanish Steps, and after that we were getting back on the bus and heading up to Assisi.

I'd already decided I wasn't going to Assisi. I was sick of everyone and didn't think I could take any more bus rides. I packed up my shit but kept it with me.

I still felt a bit off after the LSD. Everything hadn't quite settled yet. I was kind of glad in a way. I liked being unsettled.

Anne caught up to me as we walked over to the Spanish Steps.

"Feeling better?" she said.

"Yeah." Then I said, "Sorry I slammed the door on you last night."

She laughed. "I don't care."

I didn't really like the way she said that.

"Why do you have your backpack?" she said.

I told her I wasn't planning on going to Assisi.

"How are you going to get back?"

"Train, I guess."

"I'm really looking forward to seeing Assisi," she said.
"Cool," I said.

Red beard man gave another spiel at the Spanish Steps.
Apparently they were called the Spanish Steps but they
were put in by a bunch of French guys. Go figure.

Then he started talking about Keats, who had died in
the pink house right off the Spanish Steps. I guess Keats
had hoped that the Rome air would cure him from
whatever disease he had, but obviously it didn't work out
like that. I'd had to memorize Keats "Ode on a Grecian
Urn" for this class at Davis. It was actually a cool poem.
Seriously.

Red beard man took us into the pink house. We walked
into this little room where Keats had died. It was the
actual room, but the furniture was a recreation of what
Keats had at the time. Apparently some people burned
all of Keats stuff after he died.

I don't know why—maybe it was the lingering effects
of the acid—but I was looking at the recreation of Keats'
little writing desk and I felt like I was going to cry. Keats
hadn't been much older than me when he died. I mean,
shit, I could be dead in five years, too. But I hadn't done
shit. I was just a loser, hanging out with a bunch of other
losers.

Wendy and Amy were talking about pedicures and
Gary was showing Arnie the watch he had just bought
for himself. Gary got all uptight about being respectful
in church but here he was acting like a dork. Fuck these
people. I got out of there.

I watched from the top of the steps as everyone filed onto the bus. Good riddance.

The view was pretty awesome up there. Rome was fucking beautiful. The sadness I had felt a few minutes before in Keats' house had passed. I was happy about Keats now. Live fast and die young. Hell yeah! And if you were gonna die, this was a pretty good place. But I wasn't ready to die just yet. Not before I got something to eat anyway. I was fucking starving.

That's when I spotted the McDonald's. I couldn't believe it. How many McDonald's did they have in this town? I ran down the steps.

Later, I took a bus to the train station, where I bought a ticket back to Florence. It was easy and pretty cheap, too.

It was a four-hour train ride. I mostly hung out in the walkway with the window open and scenery blasting past and Italians squeezing by from time to time. I kept burping up Big Mac.

As we got closer to Florence this American chick in red jeans walked up to me and asked me if I went to UC Davis. I said no.

Thirty-Nine

It felt weird being back in Florence. The place seemed really small and lame and quiet after Rome.

When I came into the apartment, Gina was in the bathroom, taking one of her epic baths. I went into my room and sat on my bed. Then I stood up. I never knew what to do with myself in this fucking country.

A while later there was a knock at the door. I answered it and the Germans started pushing past me with backpacks and sleeping bags.

"You guys moving in or what?" I said.

"For a while," Wolf said.

They started arranging their stuff around the living room. Wolf stacked a bunch of tubes of architectural drawings in the corner.

Gina walked out of the bathroom with a towel on her head. She didn't look all that pleased.

I retreated to my room.

Forty

The next morning I was just sitting around, bored, with the Germans. So I decided to teach them how to skate.

Johan had the wrong shoes—these weird pointy leather art shoes. Wolf was wearing Adidas and seemed pretty confident. But he totally sucked. He fell off like five times before giving up. Johan didn't seem to have any problem balancing. He just didn't want to fuck up his shoes. So he didn't want to do much more beyond just push off once or twice. Lesson over.

Back inside, bored again. Three more weeks of this shit.

I couldn't help thinking of everyone at Assisi. I was glad I was here. Fuck those people. But still. This whole Anne thing was still bugging me. I had to figure out what to do.

Things were kind of tense around the apartment. I guess Gina was pissed at Oscar for inviting the Germans to stay with us. I didn't really blame her. She spent a lot of time chanting in her bedroom while Oscar and the Germans hung out watching TV or talking quietly in the kitchen.

Forty-One

I felt like a total alien in school. It was like I had crossed some kind of line in Rome, like I didn't belong there at all anymore.

At lunch it was just me and Trish and Wendy and Amy. No idea where Gary was.

Trish said, "I have to talk to you."

"Okay," I said.

"Not here," she said.

"Alright," I said.

"Later," she said.

"Okay," I said.

I'd spent the weekend trying to tell myself that I didn't care about Anne. But that all went out the window the second I saw her in political science.

She said, "People were saying you weren't coming back."

"Oh yeah?" I said. "Why?"

"I don't know. You seemed kind of pissed off or something."

I shrugged. "How was Assisi?"

"Amazing. You totally missed out."

"Oh yeah?"

"Yeah, the Church of St. Francis was incredible."

"Cool."

"How was the train ride back?"

"Fine," I said.

"Hey, I talked to my mom last night. She said your dad's back is all messed up. I guess he's on some major pain meds or something."

I shrugged. "He's like that a lot."

"Have you even talked to him?"

"No," I said.

"You know they get here Saturday night, right?"

"Yeah, I guess."

"Anyway," she said. "I'll be back from Bologna in plenty of time."

"Bologna?" I said.

"U2."

"Oh, right," I said.

She smiled.

Trish caught up with me as I was leaving the center.

"Do you know about Gary and Anne?"

"What?" I said.

"Do you know about them? I just wanted to know."

"Know what?" I said.

"They're like, an item now."

I stopped walking. "Bullshit," I said.

"They spent the night together in Assisi."

I didn't say anything.

"Don't believe me? Ask her. Ask either of them."

And then she walked off.

I felt like someone had punched me in the stomach. I actually felt ill.

I don't know what I did then. I walked around for a while and tried to tell myself I didn't care, but it didn't work. Maybe the whole thing with my dad coming was making things seem even worse, but I definitely had this weird hollow feeling inside.

I lay around the apartment for the rest of the day in a shit mood. I stayed in my room to avoid dealing with the Germans. They were hanging around in the living room, watching TV in their underwear.

I couldn't stop thinking about Anne. Maybe it wasn't justified, but I was pissed. And jealous. I fully admit it.

Forty-Two

I blew off school for a few days. I just couldn't deal. I kept thinking about everything, but mostly I kept thinking about Anne.

The apartment was no picnic, either. I didn't see Oscar much, but when I did, he and Gina were fighting. Then one day Oscar's painting disappeared from my room. Something was up.

The Germans were still around. Or anyway, their stuff was, but it stayed piled neatly in the corner. The Germans themselves seemed to be making an effort to spend as much time away from the apartment as possible.

Gina basically kept to her room and the bathroom, where she took increasingly long baths.

When I finally went back to school everyone was gone. Or anyway, just about everyone I knew. Trish, Gary, Wendy and Amy. Arnie and Anne.

I saw Susan at lunch.

"So Anne and Arnie really went to U2?"

"I guess."

"Why didn't you go?"

"Not my thing."

Then I said, "So what's up with Anne and Gary?"

Susan rolled her eyes. "What do you care?" She walked off.

After lunch the administrator lady called me to tell me I was failing Italian. It was weird cause recently I had started feeling like I was actually getting it. I guess my Italian professor felt otherwise.

"So what does that mean, exactly?" I said.

"It means you'll get an F."

"And..?"

The lady shrugged.

I guess it didn't really mean anything.

My mom had called a few times in the last couple of weeks so I decided I better call her. So I had to kill some time downtown after school before it would be a good time to call. I decided to drop in on the chrome bar. I hadn't seen Antonio in a while. Plus, I kind of felt like having a beer.

Antonio was hanging out at the bar with some tall skinny bald dude I hadn't seen before.

"Americani!" he said. "Ciao. How are you?"

"Okay, you?"

"Fine," he said. He was pulling out some cigarettes. He offered me one. "Smoke?"

"No."

"Ah," he said. "Healthy man."

"That's me."

He introduced me to his bald friend, Giovanni.

"Pleased to meet you," Giovanni said.

"You speak English?" I said.

"He live in Texas for one year," Antonio said.

"Oh yeah?" I said.

"Yes, Houston," Giovanni said.

"Houston," I said. "Cool."

"You like the Oilers?" Giovanni said.

"They're not a team anymore."

"Warren Moon. Very good, eh?"

"Dude retired a while ago."

Giovanni nodded. "Yes, yes."

Then Antonio said, "So why you no go to Bono?"

"You knew about this?"

"Yes. Of course."

"Why didn't you go?" I said.

"Me and Wendy, no more."

"What?"

"Yes, it did not work out."

"That sucks," I said.

He shrugged. "Girls very complicated."

"Tell me about it."

Antonio stubbed out his cigarette. "So. We go now. We are meeting some peoples."

"People," I said.

"What?"

"It's 'people,' not 'peoples,'" I said. "Kind of like sheep."

"Sheep?"

"Yeah. Or fish."

"Come?"

"Forget it," I said.

"Okay," he said, patting me on the back. "Ciao."

"Ciao," I said.

After they left I ordered a beer and just sat there for a while.

I went and called home. My brother answered.

"Hey, what's up, man?"

"Nothing," I said.

"So you're gonna be home in two weeks."

"Yep."

"Get any Italian pussy yet?"

I sighed. "Where's mom?"

"You're really letting me down, you know that?" he said. "I mean, what kind of example do you think you're setting for your little brother?"

"Where's mom?" I said.

"Don's dad is sick again. They're at the hospital."

"That sucks," I said. Don's dad had Alzheimer's. Then I said, "So Dad's coming to visit in a few days."

"Awesome," my brother said.

"Yeah," I said.

My brother belched.

"So they left you alone in the house?" I said.

"Hell yeah," my brother said. "Party."

"Alright, well try not to get arrested."

"I'll try."

"See you in two weeks," I said.

"Later."

I walked outside. Strangely, the conversation with my brother had cheered me up a bit. Two more weeks.

Forty-Three

The call came Saturday afternoon. I had been out skating and when I came in Gina said, "Your father called. You need to call him back." She handed me the number on a scrap of paper.

Fuck.

I went and dumped my skate in my room and washed up and then walked into the kitchen and called the number. It was some hotel. They rang me through to my dad's room. Anne answered.

"Where the hell are you?" she said.

"What?"

"Are you coming over?"

"Yeah, I guess." Then I said, "Everything okay?"

"Your dad has a migraine."

"Oh."

Of course they were staying in some expensive palace near the Duomo. It was literally a palace—with tall arches and a bunch of sculptures and frescos and stuff. Kings had lived there. Now my dad was there.

The guy behind the desk spoke perfect English. He directed me up to the room.

My dad was lying on the bed with a wet towel over his face. Anne and Cheryl were sitting on the floor. It looked like Cheryl was doing some kind of Yoga exercise.

Cheryl got up and gave me a hug. She was all skinny and bony with her black wiry hair going in every direction. She said, "It's great to see you."

"You, too," I said, lamely.

My dad peeled back his towel. His face was kind of bloated and his skin looked blotchy. He looked like a sick goldfish.

"Hi Dad," I said.

"Hi."

"How was the flight?"

"Horrible," he said.

"Poor dear," Cheryl said. She stuck out her lip sympathetically.

My dad said, "We've been invited to Fiesole tomorrow."

"Oh yeah?" I said.

"My friend Barton is renting a villa there."

My dad's "friends" were other shrinks, and they all tended to be boring assholes.

"Have you been to Fiesole yet?" Cheryl said.

"No," I said.

"It's supposed to be very nice," she said.

My dad made a slight groan and put the towel back over his face.

"We're very tired," Cheryl said.

"I bet," I said.

"We'll get out of your hair," Anne said, giving her mother a kiss. "When should we be back?"

"We're due there at one o'clock," my dad said from under the towel. "So be here at noon."

"Will do," Anne said. And with that, we departed.

Once we got outside neither of us seemed to know what to do. I said, "So how was U2?"

"Okay," she said.

"Just okay?" I said.

"Not really my thing, I guess."

"Oh yeah?" I said. And then I couldn't hold back any longer. So I said, "So Trish said you and Gary are like the hot ticket now."

"What?" Anne said. She looked confused.

"She said you guys hooked up in Assisi."

Even in the dark I could see her face was turning red.

"What?" she said. "You believed her?"

"I don't know."

"Fuck you." And then she shoved me—pretty hard, actually. She turned and started walking away. "What an asshole."

"Hey," I said. But she didn't stop or turn around. She kept walking.

"Hey," I said. I ran after her and tried to catch her arm, but she pulled away and kept going.

I did feel kind of asshole-ish, but—I admit—happy, too. I mean, if I had to choose between Anne being with Gary or Anne hating me, I know what I'd pick. No brainer.

Forty-Four

I arrived back at the hotel at noon. The guy with the perfect English called up to my dad's room and then said they'd be down in a second. I sat on this big bench with cushions that let out a bunch of air like fart pillows. And then I waited. And waited.

Finally Cheryl came down. She was wearing tights and a huge baggy sweater thing which hung off her shoulders and exposed her pointy collarbones.

We sat on the fart pillows. Cheryl crossed her legs and pulled her sweater down to cover her skinny thighs.

"It is so beautiful here," she said.

"Yes."

"You are very lucky."

"I know."

Then Anne showed up. She barely glanced at me, so I guess she was still pissed about what I had said the previous evening. She and her mom started talking about Anne's dad. His law firm was being sued or they were suing someone or something like that.

Finally my dad came down wearing what looked like a fur coat. He shook my hand. I swear, he has the wussiest handshake. Most guy's dads make a big point of teaching their sons to shake hands in a firm, manly way. Not my dad.

He said, "We're late."

We got a cab. My dad told us where we needed to go and then Anne translated for the driver.

My dad looked at me and said, "How come you're not doing the translating?"

I shrugged. Then I said, "Is that a fur coat?"

He didn't answer.

Cheryl pointed things out enthusiastically all the way over but the rest of us were just kind of glum and silent.

The Fiesole place was a huge house with a bunch of ivy crawling all over it.

Barton was short and fat. His wife was about a foot taller than him and was wearing a bunch of purple scarves on her head.

We were introduced to another couple—some wimpy British dude and his Indian wife, who was wearing a neck brace. Then we all walked into a sunny room where a table was set for us. I wasn't hungry. I still couldn't get into the big lunch thing.

The food came and we started the first of what turned out to be five courses.

The conversation was pretty pathetic. Barton and my dad and Cheryl all talked shrink stuff. After a while the topic changed to everyone's health problems. Anne glanced at me from time to time and smirked.

After coffee we were moved to another room. I couldn't handle sitting around listening to these people talk anymore so I excused myself. Anne did the same.

We walked around a bit and checked the place out. The place was huge. We wandered through a bunch of hallways and random rooms and finally ended up in this sunroom.

I sat down on a large wicker couch. I'd had a bunch of wine to drink with lunch so I was feeling kind of tired and out of it. I started flipping through a stack of old French Vogue magazines. These were the thickest magazines I'd ever seen. Lots of naked women.

I put down the magazine and slumped back into the couch. Anne was sitting across from me.

"Hey," I said. "Sorry for being such a dick last night."

"That's okay," she said.

"I guess I was just jealous," I said.

She stared at me for a while. Then she burst out laughing.

"What?" I said. "It's true." And it was true. Fuck it.

"Don't you think it's a bit weird?"

"What?"

"Our parents are dating."

"So?" I said. "Anyway, I don't care what my dad does or thinks."

She smiled. Then she said, "How long do you give them?"

"Who?"

"Your dad and my mom."

I shrugged. "I can't believe your mom hasn't gotten sick of him by now."

She laughed. "She's pretty annoying, too. Maybe they're perfect for each other."

"Maybe," I said. "So you think it would be too weird?"

"What?"

"Us."

"I don't know," she said. Then she laughed and shook her head. "You're crazy."

Then all of sudden the lady with all the scarves was standing over us.

She said, "You might want to come to the dining room."

"What?" I said. "Why?"

"It's your father. I think it's his back."

My dad was lying in the middle of the floor in the dining room. Barton and the British guy and his weird wife were all just standing around, looking uncomfortable.

"Dad?" I said. "You okay?"

"I don't know. I think so." He wedged his hand under the small of his back and started feeling around.

"Where's my mom?" Anne said.

No one said anything for a moment. Then Barton said, "I think she's in the bathroom."

The lady with the neck brace said, "She's been in there a while."

Anne went off to find her mom.

My dad said, "I need to get back to the hotel."

I said, "You sure you don't want to stay here for a while?"

"My pills are at the hotel."

Anne came back with Cheryl, who looked a bit pale.

Cheryl rushed over to my dad, who was trying to sit up. We both helped him up.

"Are you okay?" she said.

"I just need to get back to the hotel."

Barton said, "I can drive you."

Then Barton and his wife got into a huge argument about whether or not there was any gas in the tank. Finally Barton shouted her down, saying, "I can buy gas if we need it. They do sell gasoline in this country."

We drove back to Florence in Barton's rented Opel. His wife had been right—the gauge was on empty. Barton said it wasn't a problem, that he knew of a gas station nearby.

Anne and Cheryl and I had squeezed into the back and my dad was up front with Barton. My dad let out a little whimper every time we went over a bump—and Barton seemed to hit lots of bumps.

Cheryl said, "That meal did not agree with my stomach."

"You going to be okay?" Anne said.

"Let's hope so."

The gas station was closed, which caused Barton to swear quite a bit. He pulled a U-turn and we headed off in another direction.

Anne said, "Isn't Florence the other direction?"

Barton didn't answer.

We ran out of gas on a long downhill. Barton let it coast to the bottom of the hill and then pulled over to the side of the road.

"Now what?" Cheryl said.

Barton got out of the car and started walking.

Cheryl turned to me. "Do you think you should go with him?"

I climbed out of the back seat and ran after Barton.

Barton didn't say anything when I caught up with him. He turned up a long driveway. We were walking up to a large mansion surrounded by dead-looking trees. It was the kind of place where the villain would live in Scooby Doo.

There were a bunch of people in orange parkas milling around outside. I thought it was some kind of yard crew until I saw the haircuts. Fucking Hare Krishnas! It was awesome. One of them noticed us and then they all turned and walked toward us, smiling.

Barton's Italian was actually worse than mine, so I ended up doing most of the talking. The Krishnas were really cool about it. One guy got his old Fiat 500 and a piece of hose and drove us back down to the Opel, where he siphoned out some gas. Barton tried to pay him, but the guy wouldn't allow it.

I was about to get back in the car when I noticed that Cheryl was missing.

"Where's your mom?" I said.

"I think she's squatting over in the bushes."

Cheryl appeared a few minutes later. "I feel much better now."

No one said anything as we drove back into Florence.

Forty-Five

We got my dad propped up in bed at the hotel. He took a few muscle relaxants and Cheryl took a few swigs from a bottle of Imodium. Then Anne and Cheryl went back out to look for ice.

The second they were gone I felt trapped. My dad was just sitting there, looking glum. He was sweating quite a bit. I guess he really was in pain.

"Hurts, huh?" I said.

"Yes," he said.

He closed his eyes. For some reason it reminded me of how he used to sleep in the car during my soccer games. My mom would force him to take me to my games every Saturday morning when I played youth soccer. He'd bring a folding chair and read the paper on the sidelines. It was totally lame and embarrassing so after a while I told him not to come anymore. He said he had to or my mom would be angry. So the two of us agreed that he would come to the games, but that he would wait in the Volvo. I'd come back to the car after the game and he'd be snoring in the driver's seat with the New York Times in his lap.

After a minute or two my father said, "So do you feel like you're learning anything here?"

"Not really," I said.

He opened his eyes. "How are you doing in your classes?"

"Not that well."

My father sighed and closed his eyes again. He said, "Have you talked to your mother?"

"Yes," I said.

"How is she doing?"

"Fine," I said.

"That's good."

There was some incredibly loud moped revving outside.

My dad said, "I must admit, I'm not overly fond of Italy."

"Oh yeah?" I said. "I kind of like it." Okay, so maybe "like" wasn't the right word. But I was definitely used to the place now. Just in time for me to leave.

"So you all ready for your big conference?"

"Of course," he said.

"That's good."

"How about you? Are you ready for your return to Davis?"

"I don't know," I said.

"What do you mean you don't know?"

I shrugged.

"You are planning to go back," he said. "Aren't you?"

"Sure," I said.

"Are you going to be able to graduate next year?"

"I think so," I said. Honestly, I didn't know.

"Don't drag it out," he said. "There's no point in dragging it out."

"You're probably right," I said.

"I had hoped you'd find something that inspired you," he said. "Something you felt passionate about."

I shrugged. "I'm sure I will. I just need a bit more time, I think."

"Time," he said.

"Maybe I should join the Hare Krishna."

And then Anne and Cheryl walked back in with a bag of ice. I couldn't believe it.

"Where did you get that?" I said.

"Downstairs," Anne said.

"Wow." I was actually impressed.

Cheryl started helping my father hitch up his shirt—his pale, flabby stomach was bulging out over the top of his belt. My dad started breathing in and out really quickly. Anne and I just stood there and tried not to watch.

Finally I said, "We should probably go, huh?"

"Yes," Cheryl said. "We need to wake up early for our flight."

So then we all did the hug thing.

My father said, "Please don't join the Hare Krishnas."

"I won't," I said.

Then we left.

Forty-Six

When we got down to the street Anne said, "What was that about the Hare Krishnas?"

"Nothing," I said.

"I'm hungry."

"Seriously?"

"Yeah, I barely ate anything. It was a total meat fest."

"Where do you want to go?"

"Let's go to that Chinese place."

"Serious?"

"Oh come on, you said you'd go with me. You even shook on it."

"I did?"

"Come on!" And then she dragged me to the Chinese place.

It was pretty much your generic Chinese place with the red lanterns and greasy menus and everything. Kind of funny. They poured us those little cups of tea. The menu was in Chinese, Italian and English.

Then I noticed that we were the only people in there. Probably not a good sign.

"Gotta get sweet and sour pork," I said.

"Yuck," Anne said.

"Oh, come on."

"Even if I was a major carnivore I'd still think that dish was gross. It's not even authentic."

"What are you talking about?"

"It was invented for stupid Americans."

"Whatever," I said. "It's good and I'm gonna order it."

The waiter was a Chinese dude with wispy chin hair. We ordered in English. He took our menus and left.

"So we survived," Anne said. "Hi five!"

We high fived.

"Think your dad will be okay?" she said.

"He'll be fine." Then I said, "Think your mom will last much longer?"

"What do you mean?"

"With my dad."

"Oh," she said. "Actually, she told me she's leaving him."

"She is?" I said.

"Yeah," Anne said. "She told me tonight. She said she's gonna to wait til they get home, though."

"Oh," I said.

"What?"

"I don't know." For the first time in a long time I actually felt bad for my dad.

The food came. The sweet and sour pork looked pretty good, actually. I wasn't so sure about the brown sloppy shit Anne had ordered.

"How is it?" I said.

"Good. How's your artificially flavored and colored pork?"

"Excellent."

"Do you think the flavoring comes in a bottle?"

"Who knows?"

"Or maybe it's a powder. 'Just add pork and water.'"

"Hilarious," I said.

The fortune cookies came on the little dish with the bill.

"Fortune cookie?" I said.

"You choose," she said.

"You're gonna let someone else determine your fortune?" I said.

"No, I'm determining it by letting you choose."

"Oh, I get it." I picked one and opened it.

"What does it say?" Anne said.

"I don't know. It's in Italian."

"Let me see it."

She read it and started laughing.

"What?" I said.

"It says, 'Non lasci l'occosione tramite le vostre mani.' Or don't let opportunity slip through your hands."

"What does yours say?"

"Mine says 'Avete una decisione grande da fare.'"

"What does that mean?"

"Your Italian really does suck."

"Thanks."

"It means I have a big decision to make."

"Do you?"

"I don't know," she said. "Maybe."

We were just kind of looking at each other.

"Ready to go?" she said.

"Sure," I said.

Forty-Seven

Then we were outside again. It had rained while we were inside and all the streets were wet and glistening.

"What a beautiful place," Anne said.

"Yeah," I said. "It's pretty awesome." And I have to admit, it was. I don't know why, but the Duomo was looking especially cool that night.

"Are you glad you came?"

"To Chinese?"

"No, to Italy."

"Sure," I said.

We started walking back toward her place. Neither of us said a whole lot. I was thinking about how she wasn't going to be my "stepsister" much longer, how we weren't going to be here much longer, either. It was kind of a now or never thing. And then we were standing in the doorway of her place and she was just kind of looking at me with her big brown eyes, so I decided, fuck it, and tried kissing her again. And this time she let me.

It's always hard to imagine what it's going to be like to kiss someone for the first time. Sometimes it's awkward or their breath is weird or you're out of sync or something, but this just felt right and natural.

Well, mostly, anyway. After about ten seconds Anne started giggling.

"What?" I said.

"That look on your face."

"What look?"

"Right before you kissed me."

"Yeah?"

"Yeah, you looked so serious or something."

"Sorry," I said.

"It was cute."

"Great," I said. "Thanks a lot."

"Don't get mad."

"I'm not."

She started giggling again.

"Jesus," I said.

"I'm sorry," she said. But she couldn't stop giggling.

We spent a long time kissing in the doorway. And right then I didn't want it to be anything more than that. Just kissing was fine. It was great. And I didn't care about anything.

Finally we said goodbye. And then I turned and walked back to the bus stop, burping sweet and sour pork.

Forty-Eight

It started sometime after midnight. I can't be sure because the next twenty-four hours were a blur. I've never been so sick in my life.

I barely made it to the bathroom the first time. Total projectile vomit. I barfed til I couldn't barf anymore, and then I barfed more. I barfed chunks, then moved on to yellowish bile, then to something that seemed like water. I almost barfed out my stomach lining. I managed to drink some water out of the tap but then barfed that out, too.

I woke up on the bathroom floor. Gina was standing in the doorway, looking at me.

"Are you okay?" she said.

"No," I said.

"What happened?"

"Chinese food," I said.

She wrinkled her nose. "Can I get you something?"

"No," I said.

There was a pause. Then she said, "I have to use the bathroom."

"Oh," I said. "Sorry."

I went to my room and fell onto my bed. I woke up a while later and tried to get up. I was so weak I could barely stand. I was totally woozy. I went to the kitchen and got a glass of water and drank it. Then I went back to the bathroom and threw it back up. I took another short nap in the bathroom. Then I crawled back to my room. This time I didn't even make it onto my bed. I just lay on the floor.

I woke up again sometime later. I could hear the Germans in the living room, arguing about something.

All of a sudden I wanted a Coke. It came to me like an inspiration. Coke could cure me, I was sure of it. I thought of the last Coke I'd had in Rome—how good it had tasted. I really really wanted a Coke.

I got up to go ask the Germans if they would be willing to go out and get me a Coke, but by the time I stumbled out into the living room they were gone. Shit. I was going to have to get it myself.

It took me a long time to work up the energy to go out. Finally, I left the apartment and made my way slowly down the stairs. I was delirious.

When I got outside the sunlight was blinding. I just wanted Coke. I was fucking fixated on it.

It took a mantra to get me down the street. I was chanting like Gina, but I was the little engine that could. I think I can, I think I can, I think I can...

I walked into the little grocery and wandered from aisle to aisle. Finally, I found the aisle with the Coke. They only had warm, dusty bottles of Coke, but looking at the rows of soda was like being back in the Sistine Chapel. Angels were singing. I swear it was religious.

I found a box of crackers that looked kind of like saltines, then took everything up to the register. I paid the girl behind the counter. Then I walked back out into the sunlight.

Out on the sidewalk I cracked open the warm Coke and took a sip. My lips were cracked and my mouth was all gross and pasty, but then I had that pure bubbly caramel syrupy sugary taste on my tongue. My stomach did a little lunge and I burped some carbonation out through my nose, but then everything seemed to settle a bit.

I heard a plane going overhead, and when I looked up, I thought about my dad. He was gone. And then I thought about Anne. About last night. I didn't know what it meant or where it would lead. And I didn't care, either. All I knew was that for the first time in a while I was happy.

I took another sip of Coke. I was okay. I was going to be okay.

Forty-Nine

Anne and I were sitting out on that dam thing in the middle of the Arno. It was freezing cold and raining a bit off and on. But we were both flying home the next day, so this was our last chance to do this.

"I can't believe you passed Italian," Anne said.

"Why not?"

"Your Italian sucks."

"So?"

"You must have cheated on the final."

"What?" I said. "No I didn't."

"Right," she said.

A seagull flew by and took a crap in the water just a few yards away. Or meters. Whatever.

"Think you'll ever come back?" Anne said.

"To Italy?"

"To Florence."

"I don't know," I said. "It would be kind of weird, don't you think?"

"I don't know."

"Yeah, it would be too weird," I said. "I'm never coming back."

"Never?"

"Never," I said.

"Not even to show your kids?"

"Kids?" I said. "Who said anything about kids?"

"I can see you with kids."

"Okay, now you're freaking me out."

Anne laughed. She started to shiver violently from the cold.

"We should get out of here," I said. "You're going to get exposure."

"It's not that bad."

"Seriously, your lips are turning blue."

"Okay, okay."

We got up and made our way back to the bank. Then we climbed up the steps to the roadway above. We turned to take our last look at the dirty brown water.

"I think I'll come back," Anne said. "Someday, anyway."

"Cool," I said. "Send me a postcard."